The
Canardly

Kathleen Olson

Published in the United States of America

ISBN 979-8-9998996-3-7 (SC)

ISBN 979-8-9998996-5-1 (HC)

ISBN 979-8-9998996-4-4 (Ebook)

For Book Rights Adaption and other Rights Permission. Call us at toll-free **601-914-6178**.

Table of Contents

Chapter 1 1

Chapter 2 14

Chapter 3 22

Chapter 4 29

Chapter 5 32

Chapter 6 45

Chapter 7 56

Chapter 8 61

Chapter 9 77

Chapter 10 93

Chapter 11 114

Chapter 12 121

Chapter 13 127

Chapter 14 133

Chapter 15 145

Chapter 16 161

Chapter 17 177

Chapter 18 185

Chapter 19 188

Chapter 1

"Did you get the mail this morning?" Roy shouted to his wife who was in the kitchen.

"No," she shouted back. "Last time I looked it hadn't come yet."

"Then I'll take a look," he said in his normal voice.

He opened the front door and walked the two steps to the mailbox. The hatch door squeaked irritatingly when he opened it.

"Gotta do something about that," he muttered.

Roy O'Malley reached inside and pulled out a handful of letters, a magazine and a small package. Three of the envelopes were from charities, pleading for him to be generous and donate. He had answered one of those letters positively two years ago, and now he received a minimum of two letters from different foundations every day. He sighed. And tossed them aside.

One letter, however, although it looked almost like another plea for money, was different. Its return address was from Forefathers, Inc. This he had been waiting for.

Roy took the mail into the dining room and dumped everything on the table except that one letter which he whisked away to his office. Several weeks ago, he had sent an application and a container of his saliva to Forefathers, Inc. for analysis.

A bit of spit didn't seem to him to be enough. Rob had expected to have a biopsy or something horrible like that. He just hoped the company had come up with what he was hoping for: proof that he was 100% Irish, or even 90% was okay with him.

He slit the envelope open carefully, slowly to stretch the anticipation as long as he could. Inside were several pages which Roy gingerly drew out. He unfolded the pages, leaned back in his chair, and began to read.

Within a few minutes, he dashed the papers on the floor and swore. That letter was a lie! There was no way! His parents had confirmed his "Irishness," and he had always taken pride in St. Patrick's Day, even marching in the parade with several other pure-bred Irish. Or so he thought.

Snatching up the papers from the floor, Roy scowled at the statistics printed plainly on the sheets. According to this, he had no Irish in him at all! Sure, his great, great grandparents had sailed from England to America, but that was because the ship sailed from Belfast where his family had boarded, then stopped at Southampton and took on the "real" passengers. These were the ones who could afford first class tickets. His ancestors sailed in third class.

The letter also informed him that not only was he not Irish, but rather Italian, a dab of French, a bowlful of Spanish, and a good hunk of English. This all added up to the mishmash of Americans. Roy was devastated. The solidarity he felt from being Irish crumpled. He was now spread out and undistinguished as a pat of butter melting into hot toast. Sure, it was tasty, but ordinary and predictable. Roy was not predictable. His heart told him he was fully Irish, not just a pat, but the whole stick of butter Irish.

Grabbing the letter, Roy ventured out of his office and into the kitchen where Sally was making lunch. He grabbed his wife around the waist and kissed her soundly.

"Well, where did that come from?" Sally asked with a dreamy smile.

"It came from where I come from."

"Again, please?"

"I got the results from the Forefathers, Inc."

"I'll bet it didn't say much other than you were Irish," Sally ventured.

"I wouldn't bet on that."

"What do you mean? What else is there for you, Mr. O'Malley?"

"Oh, I don't have a cell of Irish blood," Rob confessed.

"That can't be right. I've heard all the stories from your parents, and with you in the St. Patrick's Day parade, and—"

"Apparently that was all they were, stories. Most of my family comes from England. I'm also French, Spanish, and Italian. In other words, I'm a canardly."

"A what?" Sally said backing away.

"You know, a mutt, like our dog, Dusty."

At the sound of his voice, Dusty obediently came over and Rob mussed his head.

"I, I don't understand, Roy. What does Dusty have to do with anything? Yeah, he's a mutt and we have no idea what makes up his breed, but what's a "canardly?"

"You canardly tell what he is," Roy said with a wry smile.

"Oh, you!" Sally tried to say while laughing which ended up with a coughing fit.

3

"You see? I had no idea what breeds made me any more than what Dusty is. Therefore, I am a canardly," he said bitterly. "I so wanted to have a confirmation that I am all Irish, but I was royally shut down. If you think you are all Swedish, we had better get your genes investigated as well."

"I know that I'm part English, Welch, and Scots, but mostly Swedish. When I married you, I was a Worthington, my mother was a Morgan, and my grandma was a Campbell," Sally related. "But before then they were mostly Swedish. That's what I have heard, anyway. I think I am talking myself into spitting into a capsule and mailing it to that ancestor service."

"Won't hurt. My problem was that I was sure I'm Irish. For heaven's sake, I know the folklore, the people, the history, the conflicts, and the leaders. Now I must start looking into other civilizations. You know, I'm just a little afraid."

"Of what?"

"I don't know," Roy confessed, but he put a determined look on his face and announced that he was going to start looking into his ancestor's realms and see what was going on there.

"Roy, you're the writer, and I know how you love to do research. Here's a new challenge, and possibly a new book."

"Maybe you're right," Roy said thoughtfully as his ebullient spirit was beginning to take over. "That turns everything around. Watch out, Wikipedia, here I come!" With a clear mind and an enthusiastic spirit, Roy retreated to his office.

Of course, his office consisted of his computer and desk, but also tons of cabinet spaces and bookshelves. As a result, there were papers and books everywhere as Rob was not the neat freak his wife expected him to be. Oh, he put all the right papers in the right folders but then left the folders out until they had dust on them. But in this case, he was so exhilarated about the new project that he felt a need to clean up, dust off, file, shelve, and otherwise organize his space, or he felt nothing would ever get done.

It took him a couple of hours to whip everything into shape. When it was done, he looked around at his efforts and congratulated himself on making a place to work on this book and concentrate on his project.

Sally came in with a cup of coffee, stopped, and said, "Roy, what on earth did you do to your workspace? You seem to have some now."

Roy grinned. "Didn't think I had it in me, did you?" Sally shook her head in response. "The way I figure it," he continued, "that if this project is what I think, I'm going to have papers all over the place with just this. I didn't want to bury all my other books, so I catalogued everything."

Sally set the coffee on the big empty of his desk. "I'll let you alone so you can create and mess up this place all over again."

"Thanks, Babe."

He sat back in his chair and stared at the empty screen. And stared some more.

"Time for the old outline," he thought. "But how do I start? I no longer have an Irish side. Maybe I'll start with the Italian lineage."

"That's why I can't start!" he said pounding on his desk. "I don't know any names or dates, just percentages. Think. This is where your love of writing comes in. If you can write all those 'Douglas McKenzie' mystery books and make up plausible characters, you can do it now."

Roy was actually relieved. This was not the genre he wrote in, there were no characters unless he provided them. But with whom should he start?

"Okay," he said rubbing his forehead, "how far back in history can I go? I could go back as far as the invention of the wheel in Mesopotamia. About 3,500 years ago. That's no good. I have no idea what the people were like, nor could I find out and be comfortable with the characters. I need to go ahead in time when civilization ruled."

He started making a tentative outline and began to write.

* * * * *

6 BC

The lambing season was cold that spring. At least that's what the several people who would talk to him had said. As a Roman soldier, Lucius was not favored in the eyes of the Jews, but he did have an infectious humor about him that eased the people's fear of soldiers. Or at least fear of him. So, some people talked to him, and even one or two who sought him out. Socializing with the locals was discouraged by his Centurion. The Romans were conquerors, after all, who might be called on to punish any one of them for breaking the enforced laws of Rome.

Lucius joined the emperor's forces several years ago with glory in his mind. He could imagine himself as a hero of a vicious sea battle, or the conquering of a besieged town. And after all that, where did he end up? In the hot, dusty sinkhole of the Roman Empire, Jerusalem. He got along with all the other soldiers and even his Centurion on occasion. He really wanted to get to know the locals, but not as a soldier. He had no idea how he could accomplish that. So, he hung loose, listened to conversations, and talked not at all unless spoken to.

The chill of that spring penetrated his uniform armor. If this had been normal for the area, Lucius would have been glad he hadn't been in Jerusalem in the winter months.

When not on duty, he imitated the locals and wore one of their cloaks to keep the cold out. The others laughed at him, but he just smiled as they shivered in their uniforms.

"You look like one of their shepherds, Lucius," remarked Pintilius, his best friend in the service.

"And you look cold," Lucius countered. "I'd rather be silly looking than rattling in my armor like you."

There was an idea. He could imagine gathering the garb of the shepherd around him and going out in the fields and talking to the Jews almost like brothers.

But he shook his head to wipe out all the crazy thoughts. Without being noticed, how could he stockpile the clothing, much less wear it out of the barracks, and find a means to get wherever they would accept a strange shepherd in their midst.

Ah, how wonderful daydreams were!

Of course, that didn't stop him from his fantasies. After all, he knew quite a bit of their language, the customs, and their day-to-day way of living. That still wouldn't cover up the fact that he was a Roman soldier. His accent, his conqueror's attitude, and, most of all, his clean-shaven face, were dead giveaways. His ideas were truly a fool's paradise. He had the same thoughts when he had been in Gaul, and he had had the same fond hope of getting to know the people there, but again, his friend Pintilius kept him from making an idiot of himself. He was a Roman soldier, and he would always be. He had to keep the honor of Rome strong.

That spring, along with being a chilly one, was different. At least that's what the locals said. There was something in the air that they "couldn't put their finger on." It was almost, they said, that they could see "joy" over the other side of the hills, and it was coming. Lucius was even more intrigued with their myths and traditions, and his pipe dream was gathering strength. He didn't know why he wanted to know these people on an even basis, but it was something he knew he had to do.

So, Lucius began to scheme.

One of the locals that would talk to him, Justus, was his first thought. He and Justus had had several conversations about the ways of the Jews, and he was intrigued. Caesar Augustus had ordered that all the Roman world would be counted, and Lucius asked Justus how he felt about Rome and its laws.

"How do the Jews feel about having to go to their birthplace for the census?"

Justus looked at Lucius with a deep hurt in his eyes. That was all Lucius had to see to know the answer.

But now there was a real need for Lucius and Justus to widen their friendship, and Lucius explained it to him.

"I've heard your wise men say that a feeling of joy was coming to this land," Lucius explained, "and I want to be a part of it."

Justus stroked his graying beard and said, "I understand how you must feel about being a Roman soldier. You're isolated from us even when you're not on duty.

And if it is true that a bit of joy is coming to us, why wouldn't you want to be a part of it?"

"I was mostly interested in just sitting with a bunch of men, hearing their conversations and ideas," Lucius explained. "Now I want to be a part of what everyone is talking about. But how can I do that if no one knows the where or when of this coming 'joy'?"

"I so wish I could guide you, but the whole thing is so far beyond my people's understanding."

"Maybe I should just go back to the idea of sitting and listening to a bunch of Jews, and what they have to say," Lucius conceded.

"But how are you going to accomplish that? You sit down with them wearing your Roman garb and beardless face, and they won't have anything to do with you."

"I know, I know," said Lucius hanging his head. "And the more I learn about the Jewish ways, the more I'd like to help ease the hurt that Rome has inflicted."

"Then we must find a way. Let me talk to my brothers and see if there isn't something we can do for you," Justus said agreeably.

It wasn't until a week later that Lucius met again with Justus.

"I think I have a way for you, my friend," Justus said excitedly.

"What? How?"

"Matthias, who is my brother-in-law, has a friend whose uncle is a shepherd. His name is Helem, and, like you, he is curious about the enemy and would enjoy a bit of give and take to see if there is a way that there can be a neutral ground between soldier and citizen. Two things are against you two meeting: first, he cannot speak anything but his native tongue, and second, he is terrified of being in the presence of a soldier since one of them cut off his left hand, but he desperately wants to try to meet with you to help alleviate some of his fears. Are you up for that?"

"It's quite intriguing," Lucius said thoughtfully. "But what am I going to do about my lack of a beard?"

"All of the other shepherds know about Helem's desire to talk with you, and they all know you are a soldier. Perhaps you will have an audience."

9

"Of course, I'll do it! It's the one thing I have desired since I came to this unfortunate place. When?"

"Tomorrow night, if that works for you," said Justus hopefully.

"It does!" Lucius said excitedly. But then reality took over. "How am I going to get to the lambing fields in my uniform? Or out of the barracks in the shepherd's cloak?"

"Easily enough," Justus assured him. "I will send my son to the barracks, and he will pretend to accept the clothing as a charity. Then, you can stop at my dwelling and change."

"Why are you willing to do all of this for me?" Justus asked. "What do you get out of it?"

"Hope, my friend, just hope."

The transition from soldier to shepherd was seamlessly made the next evening. Lucius was so excited he was sweating under the cloak on that cool night. He was unsure how he was going to find Helem, but Helem found him. He ushered Lucius to the edge of a field by the town of Bethlehem. Despite the darkness, he knew by the smell and the sounds it was near a flock.

Lucius was invited to sit down on the grass while others gathered around him. Off in the distance, he could see two shepherds standing, guarding the flock. One of those gathered spoke enough Latin for Lucius to make out, and he used his poor Aramaic. They talked into the night.

Around midnight, Lucius noticed the full moon seemed to be getting brighter, and the others, he observed, were getting uncomfortable. Without warning, an angel of the Lord appeared to them, and the Lord's glory shone all around them. The shepherds went from uncomfortable to terrified.

But then the angel spoke and said, "Don't be afraid because I bring you good news of great joy that will be for all people.

On this day, a savior has been born to you in the town of Bethlehem: he is Christ the Lord. This will be a sign to you, and you will find the child wrapped in cloths and lying in a manger."

At that pronouncement, a great company of the heavenly hosts appeared with the angel, and they praised God and said, "Glory to God in the highest, And on earth peace to men on whom his favor rests."

Then the angels left.

Most of the shepherds were still shaking when Lucius said, "Let's go to Bethlehem and see this thing that has happened. The one the Lord told us about."

When they had found the child and his parents, Lucius was struck with a wonderous feeling he had never experienced before. He and the shepherds reveled in what the angel had said.

Lucius now felt he was more shepherd than soldier, and it no longer mattered if he even went back to the barracks or not. His heart was filled with joy and there were many people out there who needed to know what he had experienced. Yes, he was a Roman soldier, but heaven had told him what he needed to know.

Lucius stayed with the shepherds, even growing a beard, carrying the message of the angel to everyone.

He never returned to soldiering.

* * * * * *

Roy was content with the story and was perfectly satisfied that he was able to put a Roman in Jesus' story. Most of the people he was about to write about were, of course, fictional

11

since he couldn't possibly know his family tree that far back. The best part of writing was the joy it brought him.

Joy. That reminded him of something he needed to talk to Sally about, so he left his office and went to look for her. He found her in her sunny window tending her small herb garden.

"Hey, lady," he said.

"Hey, gentleman," she countered.

"I had a thought..."

"About time!" she answered grinning as she wiped a smudge of potting soil off her nose. "Sorry. A thought about what?"

"How would you feel about going back to church again?"

"But it's been at least two years since we were there. Why now?"

"I don't know, but I got a feeling of joy writing that last story, the same way I used to feel after church. It's kind of an addictive emotion."

"But you got so tired of being asked to serve on one committee or another, and I was always asked to bake, serve, and clean up."

"You know you can always say no. Besides, your new job will cut down on the time you used to have."

"That works in the wrong direction for you. Everyone thinks that just because you don't do the nine-to-five, you have all the time in the world."

"I don't think this is the issue here," Roy said thoughtfully. "I just have an urge to park my butt on a pew and hear what the pastor has to say."

"All right if you don't mind being imposed upon. And, if asked, I kind of miss it, too. Do you think they'll remember us?"

"Even if they don't," Roy said giving Sally a hug, "we'll find a welcome there."

Chapter 2

The following days were uncomfortably warm, but the dawn showed that what was in the offing for that day was ugly. Heat, humidity and dead calm made up for one of the nastiest days of the year. Forewarned, Roy got up early and left the house at five o'clock to take his daily walk. More than one idea had blossomed in his head when he took those walks no matter what time of the year it was.

Roy put on a T-shirt, walking shorts, his running shoes and left the house. He turned left at the end of the driveway and began to walk out of his subdivision where he turned right. When he hit Meyers Road, he turned left again and made the trek to Glengarry Road, the main street of town. By the time he passed the library and made it to the railroad tracks, he was drenched in sweat and wished he had decided to take the morning off. But he was halfway, so turning back wouldn't make much sense. He grabbed his travel cup from his fanny pack and took a large gulp. Even the water seemed too warm.

He got to the local McDonald's, made his usual pit stop, and decided to treat himself to an icy cold drink. What a difference! From McDonald's he found a shortcut in the form of a side street he rarely used that led directly to Meyers Road, then down into his subdivision and home.

"How did we exist without air conditioning?" he asked Sally as he came in with sweat dripping off his nose.

"We somehow made it," she replied.

"It's pure hell out there today. I would recommend you stay inside."

"Remember when we put in the air? Sally reminisced. "I thought we could never afford that, but somehow you came through. And that's why I married you, you know. I was sure you could make me comfortable."

"Oh, piffelfarf! You didn't marry me for my money. You married me for my name so you could be 'Sally O'Malley.' Anyway, it gave me an idea for the next chapter. I have some research to do, but I think this is going to be a good one."

* * * * * *

79 AD

It was hot. And it had been almost unbearably hot for three weeks, and there had been no rain for several months. Dry, water-starved leaves clacked above him, leaving him to wonder how he and his family were going to survive if this lasted much longer. Quintus Marcus Coparius was a dealer in exotic fish, and the water resources needed for his inventory were quickly drying up. Even the aqueduct was down to a trickle. The morning promised even more heat.

As he walked along the sand that early morning, by what was left of the river Sarno, he contemplated his situation. He felt an object hit his arm near the shoulder. His first thought was that of a naughty boy throwing rocks. On turning around to see the urchin, he felt another hit his back, then his head, and before he knew it, he was being pelted by something. When he looked at the ground in the early light of dawn, he saw several ash-colored, irregular rocks, and more coming down. Quintus ran for the shelter of the nearest tree, but the rocks kept coming, and the ground was becoming littered with them.

His first thought was to get home, and the call was strong enough to ease the terror he felt from the rocks. Luckily, he was less than a mile from his Pompeian estate. When he finally made it home to the shelter of his own roof, he was quite sore and bruised. His wife, Julia, stood at the door with a frightened look on her face. He stumbled in the door, saw his wife, and solidly embraced her.

"Where are the boys? Are they home?"

"Yes, of course they are. Remember, Claudia brought them home way last night."

"I can tell you, my dearest Julia, that this is no 'storm.' It's coming from the volcano. These 'rocks' I got pummeled with are what's called 'pumice.' Vesuvius is spitting them out."

"But Vesuvius looks to be so far away. How long will it last?" she asked with a large volume of fright in her voice.

"Don't know," Quintus replied. "Could last an hour or all day."

"That means we'll be up to our necks in these rocks."

"It means that we have to get away from here."

"What? And leave all our possessions? I simply won't abandon things like the necklace my mother left me, my clothes, my..." She gasped and broke down in tears.

Quintus did his best to pacify his wife. "I'm thinking mostly of the boys. They need to have the first chance. We'll pack them up with a few things and go down to the harbor to find a ship that will take them to safety.

And, who knows? We might even get passage with the boys. Then once this rock rain has halted, we can all come home. We only want them to be safe, but it must be soon. Take a look around." Julia complied, and a visage of horror came over her face. The rocks were now at least six inches deep.

"We now have so much on the ground that just walking will be a tough fete. Let's get them going. Now!"

Julia called their sons. Quintus explained to Marcus and Gaius that they would have to evacuate, and when the notion sunk into the boys' heads, Gaius began to cry and Marcus, being the older, hid his emotions as best he could.

"But what about you and Mother?" Marcus whined.

"We'll be along with you or on the next boat we can find. Right now, it's you two that are the important ones. We'll send Felicia with you, so you'll be with a trusted friend, and she can be safe, too."

At Julia's bidding, Gaius blew his nose and wiped the tears off his cheeks.

"Come now," she urged, "we must hurry before all the ships have sailed. I imagine that there will be a lot of people who have the same idea we have."

Quintus called for Felicia and explained what was happening. She quickly got some things together for the boys and herself.

It was hard work being hit by the pumice stones and wading through six or seven inches of them, but they somehow got to the shore. There were several boats waiting as if anticipating their need. Quintus directed them to the nearest one.

"Where are you headed, Captain?" he asked.

"Away from here. But I have very little room left."

Hordes of people started coming, some asking, some demanding rides, so Quintus helped the boys and Felicia onto the ship after Julia had given them kisses. Gaius was beginning to cry again.

"We'll see you as soon as we can get passage, too," Julia reminded them encouragingly.

17

Seeing what was going on, Quintus was beginning to doubt if they would ever see their boys again. The pumice was about a foot deep now, and walking was almost out of the question, but they had no choice. It took Quintus and Julia twice as long to slog their way through the pumice as it did on the way to the ship. Things looked grim.

As they tried to retrace their steps, Julia asked, "We're not going to find a ship to take us to where our boys are, are we?"

Quintus did not reply.

When they finally made it home, they couldn't open their door. The pumice was too high. Quintus began to dig out some room for the portal to open. Eventually they got into their house, but they were bruised and sore from the pumice, and their clothes were ripped and stained.

Quintus sat down, and Julia sat on his lap. "We're all we have now," he stated. "Why don't we just go to bed? Things will be better in the morning."

"By then," Julia speculated, "maybe we'll be able to find a ship for us."

"Could be."

Quintus knew he was fooling himself to comfort his wife. There would be no sleep for them. Hours slipped by listening to the pumice batter the house, and somewhere in the early morning hours the rocks started creeping into their home, coming through windows and any other passage they could find. When dawn arrived, Quintus realized that the sound of the pumice was slowing, and he had gotten out of bed, where Julia finally was asleep, to have a look. He stumbled as his feet hit the floor as the bedroom was flooded with the greyish rocks. He had to kick and fight his way to the window where he found the house drowning in six feet of pumice.

There would be no escape. In fact, since the house was built next to a protecting steep hill, they were in even more danger from a pumice landslide.

Now awake, Julia came to his side, and she put her arms around his neck.

"It looks as if there will be no ships for us. I'm glad the boys are with Felicia. She will take good care of them and raise them well."

"And I have two strong sons that will carry on the family name, thanks to you, my dear." Julia smiled and put her head on his shoulder.

Just then, Quintus felt a change. There was a wind coming, but it wasn't a pleasant, cooling one. This was aggressively uncomfortable. From what breeze that could manage to get into the house, it was a hot wind, something neither of them had ever felt, and it was getting hotter.

Quintus' Greek slave, Perseus, came to them looking frightened and sleep deprived.

"What are your biddings for the household on this odd morning, Master?" Perseus wanted to know.

Trying quickly to think his way through what he knew was coming and what his staff should know, he said, "I think this storm is letting up. We need to start cleaning the rocks out of the house."

"Yes, of course, Master. We will all do our best."

When Perseus had gone to inform the rest of the household what was needed, Quintus took Julia's elbow and steered her toward the atrium because he knew that was her favorite room in the house. Sitting down together on a comfortable chaise, she put her head on his chest.

"We're not going to leave this room, are we?" she said with some certainty.

"I thought you loved this room. You sit by the hour here with your embroidery. I know you won't mind keeping me company." He tried to make his voice soothing, but it was hard knowing what was about to come.

It was quick. So quick that neither Quintus nor Julia realized that this was the end of their lives. The pyroclastic flow from Vesuvius blasted through their house and took every living thing with it.

* * * * * *

Roy slumped back in his chair. His hands were shaking, as they always did when he wrote something that powerful. He had almost dreaded writing the end of Pompeii, as he knew of the emotional impact. But he wrote it nevertheless, and he was satisfied with the telling. Of course, he didn't know if Quintus or Julia ever existed, but his Italian heritage percent was very small, and Roy figured that this would satisfy that detail.

Sally appeared at the door of his office with another cup of coffee in hand, just one of five others. She noticed Roy's hands.

"Either my coffee is too strong, you've had too much, or you just wrote a lopdollager of an ending."

"All of the above."

"And I won't even ask you what you were writing about, at least not until you've stopped shaking."

"I appreciate that."

"Did it come from my suggested idea?"

"I thought you weren't going to ask me about it," Rob said wearily.

"Sorry. I'll leave you alone."

"No, no, I'm sorry. You at least have the right to ask that. And the answer is yes, it's your suggestion. And it is such a great start, I think I'm going to keep going. I have a lot of ancestors to follow, not only direct ancestors, but cousins and uncles and..."

"My fault. I know better than to ask you questions, and you are worn out. Best if you go lie down for a while. It should calm the jitters."

"You know," Roy agreed, "I can't think of anything more comforting to do. As usual you know me and always know what I need. Thanks"

Roy slept for four hours.

Chapter 3

Roy looked back on his writing of the tragic and horrifying events in Pompeii and after a few phrase changes, a twist of a word or two, and a punctuation adjustment, he was satisfied. At least for the moment.

Now his problem was to try to figure out his ancestor's next probable move. How would he get to Spain, France or maybe still be in Italy? And when did England come into the picture?

He imagined it had been almost two thousand years since little Marcus and Gaius had escaped Pompeii, but Rob felt that his descendants were still based in Italy, so he began the next chapter there.

* * * * *

1344

Antonio was his name, and he had heard the call of the waves when he was just a boy. So as soon as he was able, he stowed away on a ship, leaving his parents, five brothers and six sisters behind. He felt with all those children, and plenty of brothers to take his place, that he wouldn't be missed. In fact, he felt himself a hero that he was relieving his father of the extra mouth to feed.

When he was discovered hiding behind some supplies in the ship's galley, the cook jerked him out by his arm, nearly dislocating it, and marched him right to the captain.

"Look what I found skulking in the galley behind the supplies. Don't have a clue who he is. What do we do with him, Captain?"

The captain looked annoyed. After all, he was just finishing up the job of casting off which took all his concentration, and he didn't have time for children who were running away from home.

"I don't know what you want to do with him, Pio, just keep him out of my way. Right now, that also means you."

"Yes, Sir."

Again, dragging Antonio by the arm, Pio flung him onto the galley floor.

"See what happened? See what ya did?" he yelled. "Ya got me in trouble with the captain, and we're only minutes out on an extended voyage. "What the hell am I going to do with ya?"

Antonio just sat on the floor, hoping there wouldn't be any more violence. If he wanted to get beaten, he could have stayed home.

"Yer're going to have to earn yer passage, and ye're going to have to scrub this galley, do all the dishes, and run my errands. Ya got me, boy?"

Wordlessly, Antonio nodded.

Before he had time to feel sorry for himself, he found he was too excited to believe he would actually be on a voyage, and he hoped that wouldn't change. If they wanted to, they could leave him in the first port they came to, and he would never be able to get back to Italy. But he had a secret weapon: he had a good work ethic and asked Pio what he could do first.

"Ain't nothing ya can do, boy. Not right now, anyways. In about an hour we'll have to start cooking. Do ya know anything about cooking?

Antonio shook his head. Other than what he observed his mother doing, he was vacantly ignorant.

"Well, yer're gonna to learn. And fast! Once things get rolling, they don't stop, and yer'll be up to yer eyeballs in dirty dishes. What ya can do in the meantime is to familiarize yerself with what's in stock, and where everything is. And don't go thinking yer'll switch things around. I have 'em just where I like 'em. Understand, boy?"

Again, Antonio just nodded.

"And I can't keep on calling you 'boy.' Ya got a name?"

Quietly, Antonio told him.

"Speak up, boy! Ya gotta remember that being at sea can be awfully noisy sometimes. What ya think that it would be calm like this every day? No, we run into all sorts of weather. Some that could sink this ship, and ya gotta be heard over that kind of noise. Understand?"

Antonio nodded.

"Well?"

"Yes, Sir!" he yelled.

"Ya gotta voice! Then let's get started."

Antonio found out that Pio didn't exaggerate. He was literally 'up to his eyeballs in dirty dishes.' He didn't find that daunting at all and did what was expected of him. And he amazed Pio while he was at it.

When Pio finally told him it was enough, Antonio was so tired he hardly knew what to do. He had no bunk or hammock, so he took the blanket that Pio offered and spread it out on the galley floor. Before dawn, he was wakened by a no-so-gentle kick in the ribs.

"We best be getting up. Now! It's a whole new day and we have a hungry crew to feed. Get that blanket off the floor and get yer lazy ass going."

And so it was, day after day, port after port.

* * * * *

Roy saved what he had written and closed out his manuscript. He had the unfortunate (yet, sometimes fortunate) trait of taking on his character's emotions, and now he was totally tired. He walked the few steps to the old-fashioned fainting couch in his home office and collapsed on it like a puppet without strings. He conked out for two hours.

On waking, he felt energy building up inside, and he was full of ideas.

* * * * *

Several years later, while in a French port, Pio neglected to come back to the ship. The captain had no intent to wait for him. So now it was Antonio who was the cook. He felt up to the job as he had watched Pio carefully while he prepared meals. Before he went to sleep in his hammock, (a present from Pio commemorating his first year on the ship) he noted what was put in the pot and how much of each. The two had grown to appreciate each other, and Pio had given Antonio plenty of space when he started to teach him the basics of cooking. As the months rolled by, Antonio became adroit at chopping and putting together meals. When in port, the two of them collaborated on what extras to stock up on along with the basics.

But Pio was not coming back, so Antonio rolled up his sleeves and put on Pio's apron. He put together what was planned and added a few touches of his own. It was amazing what a little pizzaz could do for an everyday dish. Proudly, he served it to the crew and presented the meal to the captain in the prescribed manner.

All he got were compliments.

Antonio went on from there and soon was an apprentice seaman. He enjoyed not being in the kitchen, even though he was at mercy of every other seaman on the ship.

Gradually, they imparted to him that they had loved his cooking, and they wished he would train the man who took on the cook's job.

Antonio had his sights set on loftier things, and after several years, he was transferred to the Aquitaine where he spent his time completing his training and was now a vested seaman.

One thing that bothered him was something the Aquitaine had that his other ship did not have: fleas. Antonio entreated the captain to have the crew scrub the ship down and kill as many of the pests that they could. It seemed that it didn't help much. Come to find out that the fleas had been living on the rats in the ship, and that those rats had come aboard at the last port. He also noted a report that the rats were dying at an increased tempo.

The Aquitaine was on an extended voyage from Gascony, and would rest in the port of Weymouth, Dorset, England. That's where the captain agreed to have the ship purged of the infestation. Simple as that. Meantime, all they had to do was to keep the fleas under some kind of control and throw as many rats overboard as they could. Unbeknown to Antonio, several of the crew were sick, and one had died. The ill crew kept up the fantasy that they were okay, but one by one they failed to show up for duty. Checking the bunks and hammocks below decks, he found the men dead or dying, and each one was covered in flea bites.

By the time they got to Weymouth, five of their number had been buried at sea, and several more were showing signs of the sickness. Those men decided they would not be getting off the ship. Walking around was painful with the buboes beginning to appear and hinder them.

The port was the last stop for the rats. With help from a few sailors, Antonio had the vermin rousted and dumped unceremoniously in the water.

The rest of the men were happy to have the port to investigate, which usually meant they would stop at the first tavern they saw for something refreshing. Unfortunately, they took fleas with them.

The pests, taking advantage of the amount of human flesh in the tavern, leapt from person to person, finding new skin to infest.

This was the beginning of the Black Death in England.

By autumn of 1348, the scourge had reached London, and by summer of the following year of 1349, the Black Death covered the entire country and Europe as well. It was estimated that about half the population of England succumbed to what it was, the Bubonic Plague. It wasn't until December of that year that it began to die down, but still taking thousands of souls with it.

Antonio could not forgive himself. It was his ship that brought the Plague to England. He should have known better than to allow those flea-infested crewmen to go ashore. Logically he knew it wasn't his fault, but he should have been more aware.

When it came time for the ship to leave Weymouth, the only ones to report on board were two crewmen, the captain, Antonio, and the second mate. All the rest were dead or dying. The Aquitaine could not function with a crew so lean, so they abandoned the ship. As it stood, they would have to wait for another ship, but that could be months, so they went about finding lodgings. And jobs. Antonio thought he could always get a job washing dishes.

* * * * *

Thankful for all the naps for which he had been able to indulge, Roy had worked through the night. He finally quit around four in the morning and headed for bed where Sally was lightly snoring.

Chapter 4

Sally was up early the next morning feeling ambitious, so she made a coffee cake, her own recipe for blueberry muffins, and double-sized apple fritters. All of these were to go in the freezer until they were needed. She also expected Roy would be up and hungry. When he wasn't, she went to investigate. Of course, she couldn't have known that he was up as late as he was, but it wasn't a surprise to her after all these years of being an author's wife. There were no such things as "regular hours."

Roy finally appeared late in the morning. He paid little attention to Sally apart from an on-the-run morning kiss. She could tell he was thinking of something else entirely, writing, as it were, in his head. The only thing she could hear him mumble was "crsclom" over and over.

What Roy was puzzling over was simple: more Italian ancestors or no more. He felt that he had done a lot with a place that had its place in his ancestry, therefore probably doing what was necessary. Now he had to find a way to get to Spain or should he indulge on the obvious next move.

"Okay, Roy, do me a favor and let me in on it. What is a "crsclom?" Sally asked imitating his mumbling.

Roy seemed to snap back to reality. "Oh, I'm just going over my options for the next chapter."

"What does your outline say?"

"It says, 'Cristobal Colon."

"What is that?"

"It's a who, not a what. You know, Cristobal Colon. Christopher Columbus."

"What's there to puzzle over? He was Italian, and every school kid knows he discovered America in 1492, and he did it in three ships."

"So?"

"That's just the problem," Roy grumbled. "He didn't discover America, he accidently ran into places like Hispaniola, Cuba, and even South America. He was sure he had found a passage to India, and even addressed the indigenous people as 'Indians,' a name that is still unfortunately used today."

"But, Roy," Sally asked, "isn't that something you can really make a great story out of?"

"Not if you knew Christopher like I do. He was a monster if you ask me. He had hundreds murdered, enslaved, or executed – even his own men. Most of that dirty work was done on his second, third and fourth voyages."

"Then deal with the first voyage only," was her suggestion.

"Oh, I could, but even the first voyage wasn't the peaceful journey history paints. Besides, the voyages of Columbus are already well-documented, and frankly the subject bores me. I think I won't even mention him."

"Where will you go from there?"

"In keeping with the report from Forefathers, Inc., I'm going to add the Spanish side of our family."

"And that will be...who?"

"I'm still working on names, but it needs to be something that not too many people are overly familiar with like they would be with Columbus."

"I can see your wheels turning," Sally revealed, "so I'm going to let you get to it."

"Have you always been able to read me like that?" Roy inquired cautiously.

"Now and then. And this is a now time. There is a fresh pot of coffee waiting for you, and I saved some blueberry muffins from the freezer. Enjoy."

Roy lifted his fingers off the keyboard and rubbed them. "Getting' old," he thought. "But I can't stop now. I must introduce Carlos's sister Teresa who spawned the first link with England." He put his aching fingers back on the keyboard and bravely wrote on.

Chapter 5

August 25, 1501

Dearest Mother,

As you know, I am on a ship bound for England. I will miss Spain, probably for the rest of my life as I miss you even now. It was on the orders of Queen Isabella herself that I am heading for my new home. Searching for a new lady-in-waiting for England's Catherine, you thought it would be ideal for me to fill that position, and through one of Queen Isabella's lady-in-waiting, Her Majesty found me to be acceptable. So, here I am. I have the job not only as Catherine's maid, but also a gentle reminder to the people of England that there is still a Spanish-born royalty involved in ruling them. I hope that I won't be spurned by the English ladies. My English is quite good, and I am aware of the customs of the English court. Pray for me, please dear Mother.

Remember that I am not alone. I have my dear dueña with me.

I will write again when I am in England and settled in a bit.

Your loving daughter,

Teresa

*   *   *   *   *

November 2, 1501

My darling daughter,

I read your letter written from your ship with tears in my eyes. I miss you terribly even though I know you will be with a person I think will be one of the greatest women in the Christian world. She is a most impressive soul. Heed her well, be quick on your feet, and speak only when spoken to.

I have been waiting and waiting for a letter from your brother, Carlos. His ship left Spain about the same time as yours did, but I have heard not a word. I didn't even have a chance to say goodbye to him, as he sailed from a port I was unable to reach. At least I was able to give you one last kiss.

I am also blessed that I have your other brothers and sisters. Little Sophia already wants to take the veil of the Sisters, and Enrique is considering the priesthood. At least I'll still have Francisco, Luis, and Bonita. All of them speak of staying here and making lives for themselves, so it looks like I won't be alone.

I'll be waiting for your first letter from England.

Your Loving Mother,

Maria Elena

* * * * *

November 30, 1501

My dear Mother,

As you can tell, I have arrived safely in England, and I am now a lady-in-waiting to Catherine. I'm sorry it took me so long to answer your letter, but it has been a hectic time with Arthur and Catherine's wedding. Since Arthur is the Prince of Wales, he and Catherine have been sent to Ludlow Castle on the border of Wales. In these few months there is much I have learned about her, and her kindness and strength make me even more glad that I am here.

But today my concern is for my brother, Carlos. Have you heard anything about his fate? It seems overly long for you not to have heard something from him or his superior. What about his leader, Francisco Pizarro? Is he back in Spain or not able to answer questions like these? I will try to find a way through Her Majesty anything that I am able, and you keep looking. I'm sure we can find something soon.

I am happy with my position, and the English ladies-in-waiting are kind and helpful to me. The places I have lived in so far have been nice, but it is so cold here that I make sure there are fires going in all the hearths, or we might all freeze our toes off.

Your loving daughter,

Teresa

April 15, 1502

My Dear Mother,

I bear news. Sad news, I'm afraid. Late last month, both Catherine and Arthur, along with two of our six ladies-in-waiting, fell ill with the sweating sickness. On April 2, Arthur succumbed to the illness. Catherine survived as did the ladies, but she woke up to find out that she was a widow. Now she was in limbo, and even Arthur's father didn't quite know what to do with her. He finally came to the decision that, since Arthur's younger sibling, Henry, who was now heir to the throne, would marry her. Meanwhile, we are living in Durham House where Catherine is being held as a virtual prisoner. And so are we. There is very little money, and it is hard to even find enough to feed all of us.

Catherine has said, "I choose what to believe in and say nothing. I'm not as simple as I may seem." Because of that unassuming sentence, I'm sure she will be a fine ambassador and not let anyone manipulate her. I take strength from her words.

Your loving daughter,

Teresa

* * * * * *

June 30, 1509

Dearest Mother,

I am very tired from the events of the day, but I wanted to write more than sleep. Catherine and Henry were married on June 11. As tiring as this has been, the coronation has been even more of a stretch for my energy. Catherine seems to be holding up amazingly well, and, at times, will give us words that will pick up our souls. Sometimes she is more helpful than her ladies-in-waiting are for her! Even the English citizens seem to have taken her to their hearts.

Since Henry is now the ruler, I should address him by his title, and Catherine by hers as well. They are King Henry VIII and Queen Catherine forevermore.

Your loving daughter,

Teresa

* * * * *

September 27, 1513

Dearest Mother,

A great honor has been given to Queen Catherine. King Henry was going to a military campaign to France, he had to have someone he could trust undoubtedly to watch over domestic matters, so he appointed Queen Catherine Regent in England that include the titles of "Governor of the Realm and Captain General." What an honor! This means that her

35

ladies-in-waiting will also be horribly busy taking care of her majesty.

On the third of this month, the Scots invaded. Her majesty charged Thomas Lovell to get an army together from the counties in the midlands. Now, I'm not the one who is one to criticize the Queen, but she chose to ride north, in full armor, when she was heavily pregnant, all to address the troops. The speech she made was a rousing one, but she was very lucky to have not had a miscarriage.

Your loving daughter,

Teresa

*   *   *   *   *

May 10, 1517

Dearest Mother,

An incident has happened that I must report to you. Luckily it did no more than scare me. It seems that there was a faction that was unhappy with the appearance of so many foreigners (or as they call them "strangers") in English jobs, especially Flemish workers, Lombard Street foreign bankers and merchants.

Being foreign-born, I was afraid for my life when riots against "strangers" began. I had to remind myself that Queen Catherine was foreign-born also, and yet she appeared most calm in the face of this threat. I tried to follow her lead, but deep down I was terrified.

The riots really began when a local alderman tried to force some young men back to their homes since they were out after the curfew that had just been announced. When he tried to arrest one of them, the others defended their friend and sent the alderman running for his life.

From that incident on, about a thousand young apprentices freed those that had been locked up, and from there on, the riot increased with the use of bricks, bats, stones, and boiling water. For that, the Duke of Norfolk's private army got involved, and things became more under control with three hundred people under arrest.

With the pleading of Her Majesty Queen Catherine to her husband, all but 13 of the participants were freed. The remaining were charged with treason and executed.

In the end, both sides suffered, and the riots ended for good. It has taken on the name of "Evil May Day."

Your loving daughter,

Teresa

* * * * *

January 1, 1518

My dear daughter,

I have been worried about you. Lately you have been starting every letter with something sad or frightening. You know, you can always come home to Spain if it is too much for you, and no one would think ill of you. I can hear the heaviness in your writing, and I can tell all is not well. Please let me know what you want to do.

I have some happy news. Your baby sister Sofia has taken the veil and is now in the nunnery. We were allowed to be with her at the cathedral for the taking of her vows. She looked radiant and I was happy to see that. This is what she has been wanting ever since I can remember. Be happy for her!

Just a note about your brother, Enrique. Since he became a priest, he has been wanting to go to some country where the Word of the Lord has not been heard and give these heathens a chance to come to know Christ. Last week he got his wish, and he is going to Africa. I do not know what part, but I do know there are savages in some places that have been known to practice cannibalism. I pray that he won't be sent to that part of Africa. He's happy, I'm terrified.

Oh, my! Listen to me: I am doing the same thing I accused you of doing: being a naysayer. I will just have to make my letters cheerier also.

Your loving mother,

Maria Elena

* * * * *

July 4, 1518

Dearest Mother,

I was distressed to hear about your reservations for Enrique. He, himself, and the grace of God will take care of him. He's doing the Lord's work, and I am certain he will continue to do so.

You may think me unhappy here, but that's far from the truth. I love England! Although the winters are cold and damp, the springs and summers are more than wonderful. When I awake in the morning, I can hear the birds singing and smell wonderful things ready to come out of the kitchen. And, I have another reason to stay here, something I have kept secret from you. I am getting married. Yes, it's true! His name is Sir Peter Wellingford, and he is the son of the Duke of Wellingford, a title he will take someday. It is frowned upon for the Queen's ladies-in-waiting to marry, but I'm not getting any younger. Peter and I had a long talk with Her Majesty. Queen Catherine is happy for us and has given her permission for us to marry. We will take our vows sometime next month. I'll try to fill you in in my next letter.

I am being called. I must go.

Your loving daughter,

Teresa

*   *   *   *   *

October 24, 1518

Dearest Mother,

I'm sorry I didn't wait for your letter to write a whole new one, but I had to tell you of our wedding. Queen Catherine wanted to give us a church wedding with a multitude of friends, lots of good food and wine, but we decided we didn't want a spectacle. We were married instead by the archbishop in the small chapel of St. Paul's. I had my ladies-in-waiting and Her Majesty there; Peter included his parents and a few close friends. It was perfect.

But I have even bigger news – I am pregnant! The baby will come in the summer. Both Peter and I are ecstatic. He wants a boy to carry on with the family name of course, and I agree, but I secretly want a girl.

Considering this news, I will have a new priority. Queen Catherine was delighted I'm in the family way, and she wanted to lighten my burden and let me have a vacation from my duties. As tempting as that offer was, I could only remember Her Majesty riding to the troops in full armor to give a speech all while quite pregnant. I could do no less than she could, and I turned down the offer. She was quite surprised but agreed only if I did the lighter duties.

Peter is calling me.

Your loving daughter,

Teresa

* * * * *

December 14, 1518

My dear daughter,

I am more than pleased to hear you and your Peter were married. I wish I could have been there. I imagine it was intimate and romantic. How lovely for you!

But I am over the moon to know you are going to have a baby. Ordinarily, I would be concerned about your pregnancy and the work you do as I know it can be quite physical at times. But I did forget your Queen's personality. You are so fortunate she is there for you as you are for her.

I heard from Enrique a few weeks ago. He is still in Africa and says he has found a nice home there. He is living with a tribe that is peaceful and gentle. They like to dance and sing their songs around a fire, but he has introduced some hymns to them (the most lively he could find) and they sing them along with their own. He says it's too bad they don't really understand them, and he is trying very hard to learn their language. Once he does, he writes, he will start telling them stories from the Bible as he would to a child. In many ways, these people are more childlike than he expected.

I must close now. It is late and the lamp is burning low.

Your loving mother,

Maria Elena

* * * * *

July 22, 1525

Dearest Mother,

I am sure I have written about the other ladies who attended the Queen, but I'm afraid that list is going to change now, and I am more than angry about it. I'm used to ladies occasionally coming and going, but for three of us (Alice, Miriam and me) who have been with Her Majesty for as long as I have – can you believe it's been 24 years? — we have kept to ourselves, done what we were told, and were rewarded handsomely. But one among us has betrayed Queen Catherine. I think I have mentioned her before, I'm sure. Her name is Anne, and King Henry has fallen in love with her and is questioning the legitimacy of his marriage to Queen Catherine. He says that he should never have married her as she was his brother's wife. According to what he found in the Bible, if a man marries his brother's wife, the marriage will be cursed. And there were no sons born to them, just a daughter, Mary. And King Henry wanted sons!

Your loving daughter,

Teresa

* * * * *

December 4, 1530

Dear Sister,

As you know, my life has revolved around the Church, along Queen Catherine's life, and it has brought me peace. Since my husband, Peter, died, my life became confused and, at time, terrifying. But the queen, in her quiet but firm way, pointed me in the right direction. Peter left me the biggest gift than any man can bestow, and you know I'm talking about our two boys, Edward and Andrew. Now that they have families of their own, I can only sigh, sit back and relax. I hope they will have an opportunity to go to Spain one day and see my homeland. Queen Catherine was kind and generous to allow me to marry. I just had to promise that I would be back with the other five ladies serving her during the day.

Have you any news of our rather wild brother, Carlos? I know mother was always worried about him and the friends he kept. Although you would probably hear something before me, I would appreciate any information you can pass on.

This is possibly my last letter to you as I feel my time is coming. Despite being "imprisoned" from time to time, I have been happy here in England.

Teresa

* * * * * *

1531

Carlos knew the story of his ancestor, Antonio the sailor, who unknowingly brought the Black Plague to England and consequently the whole of Europe. Strangely enough, Antonio didn't die from the Plague like most of his shipmates, but he was left stranded in England. He did the best he could to take care of himself by doing odd jobs such as washing dishes and shoveling dirt, all the while checking the waterfront for a trip back to Italy. When no such voyage appeared, he began to check ships that didn't ordinarily take passengers, and he finally found one that headed east. Without really knowing where it was going, he booked a passage. The ship was a cargo vessel, and the only thing he had to sleep in was a hammock with the crew. Antonio had the option to sail as a member of the crew and earn a few pence, but he decided he didn't want to be bothered with such. That made him the lone passenger on the *Arrowline*. It suited him just fine.

What didn't suit him came clear three days out. The *Arrowline* was not bound for Italy or anywhere near it. The farthest he could go was Spain. Antonio landed in Spain, got a job as a printer with a recommendation from the captain of the Arrowline. And so, Antonio made a life for himself in Spain that included a wife and six children.

But Carlos wanted none of that life, nor did he want the life that his parents laid out for him. Doctoring wasn't for him. He wanted a life of adventure, to see exotic places and meet people so different they had never heard of God, the Lord Jesus, or the Virgin. He felt a need to show these different people the way of the Cross, to give them the peace that he had.

A friend of his, Bernardo, felt the same way. Sort of. He wanted adventure and the exotic places and people, but he also wanted the riches. He had heard of Francisco Pizarro and his trips to Peru, but his lust was for gold, not souls. "Maybe," Carlos thought to himself, "I can influence him to my way of thinking, so he won't light up just at the thought of wealth." But then he considered, "Maybe some of his greed might wash on me." Despite these thoughts, he approached Bernardo about the subject.

"Ay, Carlos!" Bernardo exclaimed. "I have been thinking of asking you about going with Señor Pizarro on his next voyage. Did you know the Queen gave him the rights to go and conquer Peru?"

"Oh, I heard more than that," Carlos answered with a hunk of Bernardo's enthusiasm. "I heard from Señor Gomez that the Incans are very primitive. They don't' even have a written language! They've never had beasts of burden, don't know a thing about the wheel, and have never worked with iron or steel. Can you imagine what their cities look like? Probably

43

just piles of stones. The one important thing they have is people, warriors. They have thousands of guerreros, and we can only bring what men Pizarro can fit on his ships."

"He must have used Encanto on their king!" Bernardo declared. The two friends laughed and began to make plans to sign up on Pizarro's ship. And they did.

* * * * * *

"There! That does it. I have the Italian/Spanish/English connection." Roy said out loud. Wouldn't it be wonderful, he thought, if that were the real way it happened. However, the Forefathers, Inc. doesn't mention anyone's job, so I imagine jobs for them. I've always had a place in my heart for Queen Catherine, the way she stood up and insisted she was the true and rightful wife of Henry VIII.

True to his habits, Roy, exhausted by the emotion he put into his work, fell asleep. Unfortunately, he fell asleep in his work chair, and by the time Sally woke him up, he found himself bent over forward, his head almost touching his knees. She helped him straighten up and pointed him in the direction of their bedroom.

"What time is it?" he groggily asked his wife.

"It's just past eight, so you can just relax and go to sleep for the night. I'll be along just a bit later. I think we both need a heap of rest," she said as she helped him get ready for the night.

Roy vaguely remembered something else being said, but he didn't remember what as he slipped into a sound sleep, this time without Catherine of Aragon and her ladies weaving their way into his dreams.

Chapter 6

The next morning Roy was up early, and when he went into the kitchen, he found Sally had beaten him there. Delightfully, she had a fire going in the old fireplace they had in the kitchen. It was one of the features that attracted them to their 1765 Colonial house.

"What's with the fire, Sal Pal?" he asked using his favorite nickname for her.

"It's cold and cloudy outside. I thought this might lift our spirits. The trees are in full color, but in this weather, they don't have the cheerful brightness we love. Even though a fire in the fireplace won't make up for the lack of the glowing hue we hope for this time of year, at least it will make staying inside cozier."

Roy stood in front of the fire and reveled in it.

"You're so right. It's kinda like a blanket you can wrap yourself on a day like this. I wish I had a fireplace in my office. Maybe it would heat up my writing."

"Something go wrong with the book?"

"No," he confessed, "it's just a bit of writer's block. I got to where I wanted to go, and when I got there, I felt like I was on the edge of a great chasm: one more step and I'd go over. I just need a small push, a word, a sight to get me going again. I might just spend the day in my chair in the living room."

"Now there's a wasted day! Remember the Lord gave you just so many days to create."

"But I need that phrase or picture to give me momentum."

"What you need," Sally spoke like a general talking to her troops, "is to sit in your chair in front of your computer and dive into your research. That's where your next inspiration is going to be."

"Yes, ma'am, I know."

"Then get going, soldier!"

"Right away, ma'am!"

Reluctantly, Roy left the warmth and security of the fire and went upstairs to the somewhat cold office and began to look around for that momentum he had spoken about. He went through his notes, but they applied to all the things he had already covered. And he thought of Sally's foresight in having that fire. He wondered how long the fire would burn and if it lasted longer than the day, what would he do with the embers when he chose to go to sleep.

*　*　*　*　*　*

The London Report Sunday, 2 September, 1666

Fire breaks out on Pudding Lane

By Daniel Elliot

Thomas Farriner must have been very tired Sunday night, so tired that he neglected to bank the fire in his bakery oven at 23 Pudding Lane in London. This error was the prime suspect that started what could be a great conflagration. When the family found itself trapped upstairs over the bakery, they climbed into a window to the house next door. The only person not to escape was the maidservant who was too frightened to try. She became, hopefully, the only casualty.

After an hour of neighbors trying to help quench the fire, the parish constables arrived and announced that to stop any spread of the fire, the adjacent houses had to be torn down. Of course, this led to protests, so the Lord, Mayor Thomas Bloodworth was called in.

It was later recognized that he was incapable because he had taken the job to be a yes man and had no real skills in dealing with emergencies. Meanwhile, nearby houses were burning, and the flames were headed for the flammable stores and warehouses on the riverfront. Bloodworth, unable to be effective with orders he didn't know how to utilize, grabbed a hook, and began to help the fire brigade to pull down houses, but the flames were faster.

People reported a high wind about mid-morning on Sunday. This caused the ones trying to help extinguish the fire to abandon the effort, and they fled. One could see a vast humanity carrying their worldly goods, hurrying to avoid the flames. Some even stowed their possessions in local churches away from the direct path of the fire. The narrow streets of London couldn't handle all the evacuees while still leaving enough room for the fire brigade to get through to do their jobs.

The fire was a raving mad torrent by Sunday afternoon, so violent it created its own weather that spawned a huge uprush of flames into the chimney effect wherever it found a tight place such as the space between jettied buildings.

By Sunday evening, the fire had traveled 500 meters along the river and was pushing toward the city center. Because of this unstoppable spread, it was called "the most damaging fire to strike London in living memory."

The London Report Monday, 3 September, 1666

Fire Pushes on to London Bridge

By Daniel Elliot

Because of Sunday's high winds, the unchecked fire spread to the west and to the south. However, it was mostly quenched by the river there. Unfortunately, it had spread to the houses on London Bridge and was threatening to cross it and endanger the south bank borough of Southwark. Often a way of controlling any destruction was by using explosives or fire hooks, but this was delayed for hours by the Lord Mayor's lack of leadership and failure to give necessary orders. It was seen as a fatal political mistake.

Water to fight the fire was hampered. Although, in principle, there was water there from a system of wooden pipes, and by way of a high-water tower in Cornhill that filled itself from the river at high tide, this system supplied 30,000 houses. Near a burning building, it was often quite possible to open a pipe and connect it with a hose or spray. It also could be used to fill buckets. To fight the bakery fire, which was close to the river, there should have been double lanes of firefighters passing buckets to save the business and other close buildings. Since this did not happen, a monumental number of citizens grabbed what they could and fled, adding to the humanity already trying to escape the flames and crowding streets even more so firefighters couldn't get through.

Again, because of a delay, the supply of piped water was eradicated as flames got through to the riverfront and set on fire the water wheels under London Bridge.

Near to collapse, Bloodworth was found trying to coordinate the firefighting, plaintively crying that he was pulling the houses down, but the fire was faster. Bloodworth refused James's offer of soldiers, then went home to bed. When King Charles II took the royal barge to have a closer look, he found that none of the houses had been pulled down, contrary to what Bloodworth had said.

By Sunday afternoon, a raging firestorm resulted from the winds that created its own weather. Wherever constrictions narrowed, such as the narrow space between jettied buildings, the fire, fueled by strong inward winds, grew. After a journey or 500 meters west along the river, "It was already the most damaging fire to strike London in living memory."

West and north, the fire spread, but the flames going south were generally halted by the river. However, it had made it to some houses on London Bridge. Flames were threatening to cross the bridge to the south bank of the river, and the impending possibility of the destruction of the borough of Southwark. In the fire of 1633, London

Bridge, the only physical connection to the other side of the river, was dubbed a death trap. Southwark, however, had open spaces between the buildings on the bridge, and that acted as a firebreak.

To the north, the city's financial heart was reached by the fire. Lombard Street houses, owned by the bankers, caught fire. Stacks of gold were rescued in a hurry to prevent them from melting. The efforts to save the wealthy and fashionable districts were no easier than the poorer areas. The combined bourse and shopping center known as the Royal Exchange fell to the flames and was a ruin within just a few hours. In Cheapside, the opulent consumer goods shops also succumbed.

Suspicion began to flourish in London that the fire was no accident. Because of the swirling winds that carried sparks long distances to get caught in thatched roofs and wooden gutters, it was suspicious that fires were breaking out in areas that were too far from the source gave fuel to the rumor that fresh fires were being set on purpose. Because of the Second Anglo-Dutch War, it was the foreigners that were automatically suspected. A wave of street violence was caused by reports that foreign undercover agents were setting fire to houses.

The able-bodied poor found a bonanza when the upper-class inhabitants grew desperate to get out of the city. The poor hired out as porters, for inflated prices, to take the goods to safety. Sometimes the porters simply took the goods. This created such chaos at the gates that magistrates shut the gates in hope of the crowd would see there was no hope for their goods, and, out of desperation, turn to help quenching the flames.

The order on the streets may have broken down, but the King put in his brother, James, Duke of York, to manage operations. Bloodworth had apparently left the city, so James up command posts with three courtiers in charge of each post. Each had the authority from King Charles II to order demolitions. All day, James rescued foreigners from the mob and tried to keep order.

The London Report Tuesday, 4 September, 1666

The Fire's Greatest Destruction

By Daniel Elliot

Stopping the fire's westward advance was at Temple Bar, the Duke of York's command post. It was where Strand met Fleet Street that was supposed to stop the fire's movement towards the Palace of Whitehall. Making a stand with his firemen from the Fleet Bridge on down to the Thames, the Duke hoped that the River Fleet would make a natural firebreak. It wasn't to be. The flames jumped over the river and outflanked them. This and an unstoppable easterly gale, the duke and his men were forced to run for their lives.

The wide, affluent luxury shopping street of Cheapside had been breached by mid-morning. Eastward the flames moved, heading for the Tower of London and its stores of gunpowder. The garrison at the Tower had to take matters into their own hands when no word of action came from James's official firemen because they were busy fighting fires in the west. The only thing they could do was create a firebreak by blowing up houses in the area to stop the fire's advance.

With thick stone walls of St. Paul's Cathedral with its natural firebreak of a wide, empty plaza surrounding it made everyone think it was a safe refuge. However, it had been crammed with rescued goods, and in the crypt was packed tightly with printers' and book sellers' stocks from nearby Paternoster Row. To make things worse, the building was undergoing a slow restoration by Christopher Wren and was covered by wooden scaffolding. That night the scaffolding caught fire, and, within half an hour, the lead roof was melting setting the books and papers in the crypt aflame. It didn't take long to turn St. Paul's into a ruin.

That evening the wind dropped.

The London Report Wednesday, 5 September 1666

Fire Under Control

By Daniel Elliot

With the wind no longer a large factor in fighting the fire, the garrison's firebreaks began to do what was intended. Although there were separate fires, the Great Fire was quenched. Authorities admitted that coal that burned in cellars might even be burning for two months yet.

In a large public park called Moorfields that was north of the city, homeless refugees had made their encampment. The number of distressed people filling it horrified authorities. Many were without the smallest necessities, and they were living in tents and makeshift shafts. It was obvious they were living in the depths of misery and poverty. To see if there was any way they could salvage anything from their homes, most people camped in any unburned area.

As reported to the King, the mood of the people was becoming so explosive that Charles II feared there would be a throughgoing rebellion against the monarchy. Because food production had been so badly upset by the fire, little or none was available. Supplies of bread, Charles announced, would be brought into the city every day. Markets were set up around the perimeter of the encampment.

Unfortunately, fears of foreign terrorists including a French and Dutch invasion was still prominent, or maybe more so, among the anguished fire victims. On Wednesday night there was panic in Parliament Hill, Islington, and Moorfields encampment. A story started that fifty thousand French and Dutch immigrants had gathered and had begun to march to Moorfields to murder and pillage all because a light was seen in the sky over Fleet Street. This caused a frightened mob of evacuees to rise up and fall on any foreigners they just happened to come across. Trained bands, troops of the Life Guards, and members of the court pushed the refugees back into the fields. The light that started the panic turned out to be a flare-up.

The London Report Thursday, 6 April 1669

Editorial: Summation, Conjecture, and Reaction About the Fire

By Daniel Elliot

It is believed that only a few deaths resulted from the Great Fire of London, most estimates say under a dozen. However, I challenge myself with that. Are they counting the deaths that probably went unrecorded? A demise from smoke inhalation and the fire itself must have been a larger number. And what about the deaths of those in shacks without food and basic facilities? The undocumented poor seem to have escaped counting. And, of course, who can forget the unfortunates that had been born outside of the Kingdom or were Catholics? Despite being lynched or beaten to death, weren't they also victims of the Fire? I'd be willing to wager that the death toll was not of six or eight, but of hundreds, possibly thousands.

I hear it has been reported that as many as 13,500 houses were destroyed along with eighty-seven parish churches, forty-four Company Halls, St. Paul's Cathedral, the Royal Exchange, the Custom House, the General Letter office, the Bridewell Palace, and other city prisons, and Newgate, Ludgate and Aldersgate, the three western city gates. The cost of the destruction was about £10 million. Lost books alone were valued at £150,000. Surprisingly, only fifteen percent of the city's housing was destroyed by fire.

Markets, by the Saturday after the Fire, were working well enough to supply people thanks to the Court of Aldermen who quickly began to get rid of the rubble and ruins and to get food supplies running again.

Charles II encouraged people to move away from London and issued a proclamation that all refugees would be welcomed everywhere and allow them to establish their businesses wherever they chose. Another proclamation said to forbid people "disquiet themselves with rumors of tumults." Both well-said!

As an example of those who would be looking for a fall guy or whipping boy for fault in the fire, a simple and naïve French watchmaker named Robert Hubert claimed he started the fire. Despite misgivings about his fitness to plead, he was hanged. Afterwards, evidence showed that Hubert was still on a ship in the North Sea until two days after the fire started. I have researched other similar cases, all accused by those who hated "foreigners."

From February, 1667 to December, 1668, a Fire Court was set up with an aim to settle disputes between tenets and landlords. The decisions on who should rebuild was based on who had the greater ability to pay. Because of the Fire Court, cases were usually settled within a day meaning the courts weren't bogged down by lengthy proceedings, and rebuilding was not seriously delayed. The quickly built edifices were necessary if London was to recover. According to The Rebuilding of London Act of 1666, wood was banned from the exterior of the buildings. New public buildings were built on the same sites such as St. Paul's Cathedral and the fifty-one of the churches that burned.

One of the outcomes of the Great Fire I find terribly amusing was the 1667 materialization of fire insurance companies! With all the fires in London, just in lighting alone, how can one be sure that there won't be a repeat. Tomorrow. Or the next day. I expect those companies will be wiped out within a year. Such folly!

* * * * * *

Roy opened one eye. The other was weighed down by his head on a pile of papers. Sleepily lifting his head, he could see nothing but words all laid out in front of him. Sitting up, he could see those words that compiled his notes which, in turn, became his book.

"Darn!" he said out loud. "Fell asleep again!"

Anxiously he groped for his printed copy.

"Look at that!" he said volubly. I must have done that in my sleep, or..."

"Or you're just plain lucky," Sally finished his sentence.

Rob looked at his wife, dressed in her night clothes.

"What time is it?" he asked, totally confused. His eyes made a quick dash at the windows, and he could see only inky blackness.

"It's past one in the morning. Are we ever going to be in bed at the same time?"

"I'm sorry, Sal," he replied hanging his head. I'll come straight to bed if you can tell me how I managed to write these pages in my sleep."

"When I checked in with you about ten o'clock you were hard at work. Don't you remember the question you asked me?"

"About what?"

"About escaping from a fire?"

He did remember!

"And you answered to simply head for the nearest exit," Roy recalled, his memory rushing back on him.

"Come on," Sally urged, "come to bed and we can talk about that, your newspaper with the Great Fire of London in banner headlines, or anything else you want. Right now, it's snooze time."

Roy happily complied. He was relieved that his memory had come back, proud of his work on the Fire, and, he hoped, that there was really no such newspaper as the "London Report."

Chapter 7

Roy didn't sleep especially well. The Great Fire was now past, and he had to move on. This time he was moving on to something completely different, and his notes and printouts intrigued him. He lay awake thinking about how to get from Point A (the Fire) to Point B (next in line in history). He had thought very carefully about this and decided he would change his venue to the United States. But how would that work? How and why would he/she go to America? That's what kept him up.

* * * * * *

1803

The rain was incessant. John was sure there had never been this kind of weather in Missouri before, and it dragged him down. He fondly remembered the trip from Philadelphia to St. Louis, what he saw, and where his dreams took him.

But he was eighteen now, and ready for an adventure of his own. His grandfather, John Starvois, had participated in the Storming of the Bastille back in 1789, and he had heard endless stories about the raid. But that was fifteen years ago, and he had heard enough adventure stories. He wanted one of his own.

After the Bastille incident, his family became cautious about everything, and finally his father said that he had had enough, and he was leaving France. That was 1792 and little Johnny was only six. His father's ultimate goal was the new United States where no one from France could possibly be looking for him. But first they would have to go through

England. To secure their anonymity, he changed the family name from Starvois to Stark.

They had to learn English. They had to learn English and American customs. While in London, they had to give up their old way of life for a shot at the new. It wasn't easy, but his Papa brought home a dozen new words every night from his job as a dock worker. Unfortunately, the men on the dock with Papa knew what he was doing and slipped in some "improper words" as well. The result was instead of greeting her friends with "good morning," Mama innocently cursed them. After realizing what Mama was saying, Papa checked with other sources exactly what kind of words he was bringing home.

As young John saw it, Mama and Papa were living in a world he could just not understand. They spent all their time learning English and local customs, while still, in their minds, living in France. He saw them as living like that for the rest of their lives. That is, when one day, Papa came home in the middle of the day and joyfully said in English to pack up everything they could as he had a ship in the harbor waiting for them. Mama asked Papa, where was it going? He replied that it was going so close to Philadelphia that we could almost walk the rest of the way. Mama tried to look happy, but a scowl floated against her false exterior.

Too much was attempted to put in bags and sacks that were too little to carry everything. Mama had to give up her dishes and she cried. When they finally worked out what they were able to take, they left that house in London leaving all their furniture behind.

This, to young John, was an adventure! He had never been on the open seas other than the short crossing from France to England. They should be at sea for a good long time on this journey. His parents could hardly pry him away from the railing: he wanted to watch the seas, even at night.

They landed when the ship docked in Delaware Bay and caught a ride to Philadelphia. Making their way through the city, they finally came to a house where a cousin of Mama's lived. This is where they would stay until they could find a house for themselves.

Johnny was disappointed. He had lived in Paris and London, and now next to another big city. Where was the adventure in that? Apparently, Papa agreed and soon they were packing up again, this time to travel overland to St. Louis, Missouri where Papa had a friend that had worked on the docks with him in London. Traveling a little farther north, they could find a more secluded place in a town called St. Charles and still have the luxury of a big city not too far away.

The move was a joy for Johnny. Several months on the trail that was becoming a well-worn road, he had learned to identify different birds and flowers with the help of the wagon master, a large, friendly, back-slapper of a man who knew the road well and kept all twelve wagons safe. Apparently, he had noticed Johnny's interest in the local wildlife and suggested that Johnny get himself a journal where he could record the life around him and even make drawings.

When they finally got to St. Charles, they found a place to live rather quickly. Mama purchased several pieces of furniture, new dishes, and beds. Papa went out every day looking for a job. Johnny bought a journal.

Papa finally found a job in a music store that sold all kinds of instruments. Papa played flute, piano and violin, so it was a delightful position for him. But once they had what they needed, life slipped into the same routine as they had in London with one day the same as the other. Johnny wanted more adventure. He didn't know it, but adventure was about to fall into his hands.

It was a Tuesday, and Johnny had taken a wagon into town to do some errands for his Mama. At a street corner, he noticed a man holding a handful of papers, one of which he passed one to Johnny. Johnny was quick to notice the headline:

"The Corps of Discovery Expedition"

Intrigued, he read the entire flyer and found he was caught up in the idea of traveling on foot from St. Charles to the Pacific Coast. Records needed to be kept about the where, what, and who of the expedition. It was perfect for him! He even had a journal that he had not written in yet. He was so excited that he forgot all about his errands, got into the wagon, and whipped the reins against the horses' backs, urging them home.

His parents were less than excited. Mama cried. Papa made throat-clearing noises and finally spoke. Maybe a little too much, because it turned into a lecture half-way through.

English and half in French. When his Papa had run out of things to say, he finally said that going on the expedition was acceptable. His Mama cried even harder.

That night, Johnny wrote in his journal.

1 May, 1803

I have officially been given the go-ahead from Papa to join the Corps of Discovery Expedition headed by Army Captains Meriwether Lewis and William Clark. Although I am unfamiliar with either of them, it is President Thomas Jefferson who commissioned Capt. Lewis as leader. In turn, Lewis asked Capt. Clark to be a co-leader. Capt. Clark said of Lewis:

"It was impossible to find a character who to a complete science in botany, natural history, mineralogy & astronomy, joined the firmness of constitution & character, prudence, habits adapted to the woods & a familiarity with the Indian manners and character, requisite for this undertaking. All the latter qualifications Capt. Lewis has."

Needless to say, President Jefferson heartily approved of the duo.

The Corps' mission is to map the newly acquired Louisiana Purchase, and to establish an American presence before any European powers attempted the same. The president also wants us to find a westward route to the western regions and ultimately the Pacific Ocean. There will also be scientific and economic studies on the animals of the area, the plant life, geography, and to establish trade with the local Indian tribes. Upon returning, we will report directly to Jefferson that will include our maps, journals, and sketches. Since I have studied the local plants and animals and made many sketches, my skills will be valuable to the Corps. That will be my job above all others on this adventure.

Captain Lewis issued these orders to us:

"The object of your mission is to explore the Missouri River, & such principal stream of it, as, by its course and communication with the water of the Pacific Ocean, whether the Columbia, Oregon, Colorado or any other river may offer the most direct & practicable water communications across this continent for the purpose of commerce. It's quite an adventure I have invited in, and probably a long, tiring one, but it is an adventure none the less. I'm happy with my choice."

John Andrew Stark Jr.

Chapter 8

It wasn't like Roy to wake up in the middle of the night snorting and sniffling.

"Oh, fine," he said quietly so he wouldn't disturb Sally. "Another empty night. I have to find something to do that's reasonable." His thoughts came out muddled, but he knew what woke him up. Before bed he had picked up the book on Lewis and Clark that he had purchased a few days ago. Fascinating! What an undertaking that must have been! And he hadn't even gotten to the part where they had officially started the journey. Now he needed maps. Maps that had the names of rivers and other waterways, how they were originally named and their modern names.

There were sprinkles of their journals included, and Roy was half amused, and half sickened by their spelling, punctuation, and form. It was like they dropped out of school after the second grade. Spelling was by imagination, punctuation was useless, and form was non-existent. Some of their sentences were so bad they'd have made more sense if they were a witch's incantation.

He sat down in his big, comfy chair with book and paper in hand, and began to scribble notes. Most of the journals, he thought, would be Johnny's writing, or rather as he would be called, "Stark", on the trip. Like all the hands on the journey, he would be expected to add muscle as well as brains to the effort. Stark was young and full of vinegar, and Roy decided he would fill the bill just perfectly.

After a while, and with notes in hand, he went into his office to start a few paragraphs.

* * * * * *

May 1, 1804, Monday

We set off on our great adventure with cheers from people on the shore. I understand they are mostly French. Along with my duties of oarsman, boat repair, and hunter, I am to be right-hand man to Capt. Lewis as he makes notes of the birds, animals, flora, etc. We will submit both sketches of the animals and plants, and I will make the notes as to the colors, leaves, bark, formation of trees, the songs, feathers colors, sizes of various birds, and describe in detail the visage of the various animals. I don't think that there will be much of a difference when we first start out, but the end of the journey could have a whole new species of things! I wonder if I can name any of them if I am the first to discover whatever it is. I can imagine "Stark's warbler" for instance.

May 15, 1804, Tuesday

It is a fair day, and I saw a number of goslings. Nothing special. The water is excessively rapid, and it is causing the banks to fall in.

May 16, 1804, Wednesday

We arrived in the village of St. Charles. It is surrounded by coal hills making a great quantity of coal. With all that resource, one would think the village of about one hundred houses would have a good income, but the chiefly French people are poor but polite and friendly.

May 24, 1804, Thursday

According to Capt. Clark's addition to my own, we: "passed a verry bad part of the River Called the Deavels race ground, this is where the Current Sets against some projecting rocks for half a Mile on the Labd. [left] Side, passed between an Isld. And the Labd [left] Shore a narrow pass above the Isld. is a verry bad part of the river, we attempted to pass up under the Labd. Bank which was falling so fast that the evident danger obliged us to cross between the Starbd [right] Side and a Sand bar in the middle of the river, we hove up near the head of the Sand bar, the Same moving & backing caused us to run on the sand. The Swiftness of the Current Wheeled the boat, Broke our Toe rope, and was nearly over Setting the boat, all hands jumped out of the upper Side and bore on that Side until the sand washed from under the boat and Wheeled on the next bank. By the time She wheeled a 3rd Time. It got the rope fast to her Stern and by the means of swimmers was Carried to Shore and when her stern was down whilst in the act of Swinging a third time into Deep Water near the Shore, we returned to the Island where we Set out and ascended under the Bank which I have just mention, as falling in,"

I have a feeling that we are going to see a lot of failures like this, but with this crew we should be protected very well.

June 5, 1804, Tuesday

With our stocks that we bought in St. Louis almost gone, we are really starting to depend on the land for our sustenance. We were hunting buffalo and snagged a fine lot of beavers. Swimming to an island in Little Manitou Creek, Capt. Clark's negro slave, York, gathered a fine bunch of wild cresses also called tung grass. It made a fine green for our dinner.

June 17, 1804, Sunday

Although we all agree that the country is beautiful, and it abounds with elk and bears, many of the crew have boils, dysentery is common (probably due to the water we drink). As Captain Clark wrote, "The Ticks & Musquiters are verry troublesome." Joe Fields was bitten by what we think was a rattler, there are a few cases of sunstroke as the heat is getting too many in the party. It was here the Missouri turned from westward to predominantly north.

July 30, 1804, Monday

Captains Clark and Lewis went out today and came back telling of their walk on the high prairie, which is covered in grass about 12 inches high, but the soil was good quality.

One of our hunters brought back an animal I did not recognize, but he called it a badger, and the Ponies Indians called "Cho car tooch." Its head somewhat resembles a dog with short ears and a tail. Its skin was thick and loose and had a white streak from its nose to its shoulders. We concluded it is of the bear family, and we stuffed its skin. So interesting! If this is a taste of what is to come, I will be more than glad to be part of this adventure.

We saw tall timber such as cotton, mulberry, willow, elm, sycamore, ash, and linden.

August 1, 1804, Wednesday

The prairie that is below our camp is covered with a bounty of grass as high as 8 feet with thickets of currents, hazel, raspberries, grapes, and plums. What I found most interesting was the report of a variety of plants and flowers of an unknown origin. Without seeing them myself, I am unable to identify what they saw.

August 2, 1804, Thursday

A local trader came to our camp with some Otteau and Missouri Nation Indians. There were six chiefs among them. Since they came at sunset, we said we would speak to them tomorrow. Every man in camp is on guard. They are ready for anything.

August 3, 1804, Friday

Met with the representatives of the tribes that appeared this morning. A long speech was given about our journey, how to conduct themselves, and the wishes of our government. How much of it they understood was unknown. We gave them many presents, and Capt. Lewis shot his air gun which astonished them.

August 22, 1804, Friday

While examining a bluff that contained pyrites, cobalt, alum, copperas, Captain Lewis nearly poisoned himself by tasting the minerals. I told him they were poisonous, but he didn't listen, his curiosity getting the better of him. He later took a dose of salts to work off the effects of the poison.

September 4, 1804, Thursday

While the game has been amazingly good, here, as we passed the mouth of the Niobrara River, it increased abundantly. First, we saw what we called a "barking squirrel" that lived in a hole in the ground, then we saw our first antelope. But there are elk and buffalo on the hills, foxes, squirrels, grouse. Unfortunately, we also have a great number of mosquitos (or "muskeetors" as some say).

September 21, 1804, Friday

Camping out with Capt. Clark tonight on a sand bar when, about 1 o'clock in the morning, I felt half of my sleeping gear fall away. It was lucky there was a shining moon out so I could see to my horror that the sand bar was giving way. The Sgt. on guard woke everyone as the camp was falling in fast. All hands were ordered into the boats as quickly as possible. We had but a few minutes to get the pirogues and boats, and by the time we made the opposite shore, our camp had fallen in.

September 25, 1804, Tuesday

We had our first real crisis this week. We had heard of the Teton Sioux, who had earned the name of river pirates, and we had to meet them to keep going up the river. They robbed traders, and once in a great while they would allow a trader to go on up or down river. Capt. Clark wasn't going to put up with that! Our captains were prepared and not afraid to fight. The Sioux were prepared to bluff. They tried stringing their bows as a posture to attack, but the white men did not give in. When it came down to it, Capt. Clark, furious and barely in control of himself, prepared to fire the swivel gun, and Indian bluster disintegrated, and the terrible Tetons turned into beggars. The white man could not be bullied or bluffed.

At least that's what they wanted us to think.

Since our firepower was obviously superior, they realized they couldn't win by violence, so they tried anything and everything else. We gave them gifts we brought just for this occasion. We gave them medals, an American Flag, tobacco, knives, and other small articles, even a small bottle of whiskey which they enjoyed.

September 26, 1804, Wednesday

When we explained to the Tetons that we had a long way to go and must push on, they begged us to stay one more night as their women and children had never seen a pirogue. Captain Clark insisted we had to go, so the Indians began to act as if they were intoxicated. It took some difficulty, but Captain Clark got them off the pirogue, all but the head chief, and he grabbed hold of the cable and sat down. Capt. Clark ordered all the men to stay at arms.

The Tetons were cautioned that we were also warriors and could not be treated like squaws. The chief then said that if we were to go that they would follow us and kill us one by one. Captain said that one word from him would bring the whole United States army down on them.

The day was spent, and we had no choice other than to make camp that night. That's when the chief let go of the cable.

September 27, 1804, Thursday

The next morning, women and children came to view the pirogue. We found that the Indians were preparing for a dance that evening and pleaded with us to stay just one more night. The next morning, the cable on the pirogue broke and Captain Clark hollered to the men to help capture the boat. This alarmed the chief, and he yelled that the Mahas were attacking. Within minutes the banks were lined with armed warriors. This continued all day and into the night. Both Captains considered this a signal of their intentions which was to stop us if possible and rob us.

September 28, 1804, Friday

We made many attempts to find our anchor without any luck. It was with great difficulty that we got the chiefs out of our boat. All but one. He insisted that he was going to go with us for a short distance. Tetons sat on our rope. They demanded tobacco, and Captain Lewis would not be forced into anything. Stating proper reasons for them, they nevertheless did not heed. With much difficulty and almost driven to hostilities, Capt. Clark threw a container of tobacco at them, the chief jerked the rope and freed it. The boats set out but not without saying that they should stay home in peace, or we were ready to defend ourselves.

We were set to start off when we saw the bank lined with about 200 Indians all armed with one weapon or another. The chiefs said that we could not go up the Missouri any farther. The chiefs that were on board refused to leave unless we gave them a container of tobacco, which we did. Then they asked for more and then they would let us go. Capt. Lewis gave it to him.

September 30, 1804, Sunday

There was an Indian running after us who wanted to come on board and go to the Aricara's, but we refused to take on any of that band. We discovered great numbers of Indians in the hills. We gave each chief some tobacco, and we were told we were clear to go on. We did not hesitate or wait for another "invitation" to stay yet another night.

I am chilled to think that, without the skilled leadership we have, our little "adventure" might have ended there.

October 5, 1804, Friday

Set out early but heard yells from the shore. There were 3 Indians asking for tobacco. We answered them as usual but ignored their plea and went right on up the river. I do hope that's the end of them!

October 7, 1804, Sunday

Saw the tracks of the grizzly bear and they are huge. With Captain Clark, I walked up the mouth of a river and found a Wintering Camp all in readiness for the occupants to return. I killed a badger, and another man killed a black tail deer – the largest doe I ever saw.

October 8, 1804, Monday

We came to a village of the Ricaras people whose wintering village we saw yesterday. Many natives came to watch us pass. They were most astonished at Capt. Clark's black servant as they had never seen a black man before.

We met with the chiefs who informed us that the river was open, and we may depart at any time we pleased.

October 18, 1804, Thursday

We passed the mouth of the Cannon Ball River. The river gets its name from the perfectly round stones in the river.

Saw a great number of goats and our hunters killed 4 of them along with 6 deer, 4 elk and a pelican.

October 27, 1805, Saturday

We entered the Mandan village containing round houses each housing several families. Capt. Clark walked up and smoked a pipe with the chiefs of the village. Afterwards we sent them 2 containers of tobacco and proceeded on. Many came to see and hear us at the Council, but the wind was from the southwest so terribly hard that it was impossible for us to cross the river. However, many came to see the boat which they thought was very good medicine.

October 29, 1804, Monday

A prairie fire was started by accident by a young Mandan boy. The fire went so quickly that it didn't give people enough time to get to shelter and burned a man and woman to death. Several others were burned badly. A mother threw a green buffalo skin over her son that protected him from burning. The fire passed our camp about 8 o'clock and went tremendously fast past us.

November 2, 1804, Friday

Went down to the river with Capt. Clark to search for a proper place to winter. After a 3-miletrek down the river, we found a place well-supplied with wood. When we returned, there were many Indians there to see us.

November 4, 1804, Sunday

We continued to cut down wood to build our winter homes. A man by the name of Mr. Charbonneau wished to become our interpreter came down to see us.

November 6, 1804, Tuesday – Fort Mandan

The Sgt. of the guard woke us late last night to see the Northern Lights. It was an amazing sight.

November 12, 1804, Monday

The Mandans are a peaceful people and made peace with the Ricares just a few days ago, as they are seldom the aggressors. They are, however, at war with the Snake Indians and the Sioux.

November 20, 1804, Tuesday

The weather is not cooperating with our shelter-building. It snowed all day. The men are running late chinking spaces between the logs with clay. In the meantime, we stayed in the woods near the fort.

December 7, 1804, Friday

We were informed by the Grand Chief of the 1st village that a large herd of buffalo was near, and his people were waiting for our people to join them on the chase. I was one of 15 men Capt. Lewis took on the expedition. It is a tradition that a buffalo with an arrow sticking out of it would belong to the owner of the colors of the arrow. They were confounded with what to do with the animals that had no arrow.

The river is closed, the ice being 1½ inches thick. The thermometer stands at 1 degree below zero. Three men were badly frostbitten.

December 13, 1804, Thursday

The thermometer says it's 20° below zero.

December 25, 1804, Tuesday, Christmas Day

At daybreak, the swivel guns were fired with each man firing one round. We requested that the Indians do not bother us as we told them that it was a great medicine day for us. During the whole day there was dancing and otherwise frolicking that continued until 9 in the evening.

January 10, 1805, Thursday

I couldn't believe the thermometer! It said it was 40° below zero! How these people survive in this kind of weather is amazing to me.

February 11, 1805, Monday

With Captain Lewis acting as midwife, one of the wives of Charbonneau, Sacajawea, gave birth to a healthy boy. It was her first child, and it was a long, painful labor.

March 25, 1805, Monday

We saw wild geese and swans flying N.E. this evening. Everything is showing signs of spring, which is quite welcome.

March 26, 1805, Tuesday

Ice had begun to break away and nearly destroyed our canoes.

March 30, 1805, Friday

I was amazed at the dexterity of the Indians as they jumped from ice cake to ice cake to catch buffalo as they float down.

April 7, 1805, Tuesday

We have finished packing the keelboat that is to be sent back to St. Louis. It is much too large for what we have for rivers at this point, and we will continue going up the river in canoes and pirogues. We are sending back to Washington what Capt. Lewis calls "sundry articles," such as letters, soil, rock, and plant samples, (my) sketches of local birds, frogs, fish, other wildlife, and most importantly, sketches of the natives and their goods. It is a frightful amount, but the keelboat is big and can easily handle it.

We are taking with us the usual twenty-some men with the addition of the hand interpreter George Drewyer. We are also taking Charbonneau and his squaw Sacajawea who will be our interpreter for the Snake Indians.

I saw the first of the mosquitos today. Not looking forward to their visitation. But on a pleasant note, it seems that spring is here for sure as I saw maple and elm budding along with cottonwood. There were a great number of geese feeding on the new grass, and, best of all, flowers on the prairie.

April 19, 1805, Friday

The wind was so hard today we were fearful of going out in our canoes. We spent the day being lazy on the starboard side of the river. Prairies are greening and some plum bushes are in full bloom. The beavers were larger than what we are used to seeing, and there are signs of the great white bear.

April 25, 1805, Thursday

I could hardly believe it when the water froze on the oars this morning, and by 10 a.m. the wind was so high that we were obliged to stop. From what hunters have told us, we are very near the Yellowstone River. I set out on foot with Capt. Lewis and a few others. By the time we had gone 4 miles, we found the junction of the Yellowstone and the Missouri. The game was abundant. We camped 2 miles south of the confluence of the Missouri. The river has turned, and now we are on a course going west along the Missouri.

May 14, 1805, Tuesday

It happened this evening that Charbonneau was at the helm of the white pirogue instead of Drewyer. The last person who should be in command of any boat is one who cannot swim. It just so happened that this was the boat that had our papers, instruments, medicines, and everything that would make this endeavor a success. After some knuckle-biting maneuvers and an inch of water in the pirogue, we got it back to shore and put the wet articles out to dry. We are 2200 miles from our starting point, and if we had lost those articles, it would have ruined our enterprise.

May 20th, 1805, Monday

When the hunting party returned, they reported that the landscape of the country continued to be the same. A beautiful river about 50 yards in width discharged itself into the shell river on the upper side. They named it Sâh-câ-ger we-âh that means Bird Woman's River named after our Snake Indian interpreter, Sacajawea.

May 25, 1805, Saturday

Capt. Clark killed a female big horned animal. He says that this species is seen only in this part of the upper Missouri. They weighed the horns, and they were 27 pounds. The horns grew backward instead of forward and grew into two giant coils.

We survived the surprise frost from Thursday. Who would have expected to have seen ice on the oars and ice on the edge of the river this time of the year!

May 29, 1805, Wednesday

I copied from Capt. Lewis's journal as he tells the story so well.

"Last night we were all alarmed by a large buffaloe Bull, which swam over from the opposite shore and coming along side of the white Perogue, climbed over it to land, he then alarmed ran up the bank in full speed directly toward the fires, and was within 18 inches of the heads of some of the men who lay sleeping before the centinel could allarm him or make him change his course, still more alarmed, he now took his direction immediately towards our lodge, passing between 4 fires and within a few inches of the heads of one range of the men as they yet lay sleeping, when he came near the tent, my dog saved us by causing him to change his course a second time, which he did by turning a little to the right, and was quickly out of sight..."

It wasn't our usual night.

June 11, 1805, Tuesday

Capt. Lewis not well last night. We had killed some elk that we found at the point where the Rose River, a branch of Maria's River, approaches the Missouri. But before the cooking was even done, Capt. Lewis was struck with pains in his stomach that didn't allow him to eat, and, as the night wore on, the pain increased, and he developed a high fever. Having brought no medicines with us, Capt. Lewis decided to experiment with the abundant choke cherry which were stripped of their leaves and boiled until the water turned dark and had a bitter taste. He took several doses before 10 pm and claimed he was free of his symptoms.

June 30, 1805, Sunday

It is now nearly 3 months since we left the Mandan village, and Capt. Lewis is becoming very impatient. We have yet to see the Rocky Mountains and I'm not confident that we will reach Fort Mandan again this season.

July 15, 1805, Monday

In full bloom, the prickly pear is now one of the beauties of the area as well as one of the greatest pests. Also, common along the Missouri is the sunflower and is abundant along with the lambsquarter, wild cucumber, narrow dock, and sand rush. The river itself is from 100 to 150 yards across, and there is more timber here than below the Great Falls.

July 17, 1805, Thursday

Scarcely have game to be seen, but we did spot some ibex, the mountain rams with the coiled horns, the ones I described in my May 25 entry. The yellow current is now ready, and the fuzzy red choke cherry are almost ripe. Also, the purple currents. I am making reports and sketches by the armful. This is why I was hired for this adventure.

* * * * * *

Roy thought he heard a "poof!" sound and woke up instantly. He tried to clear his head to find out where he was, what day it was, and what time it was. He fumbled on the nightstand for his watch and saw it was past 2: OO, and as it was dark outside, he assumed it was morning.

It took him a few minutes to wake up enough to see he was in his office. His computer went to sleep a long time ago, and his calendar gave him approximately what day it was. Of course, he could always go into the bedroom, wake up Sally and ask her for the details, but he decided for both their sakes to let her sleep.

Trying to determine the amount of work he had done, he woke his computer and read the last entry in John Stark's journal. He remembered typing it. And he remembered doing it when the sun was out. He figured he had put in a good day's work, so he saved what he had written, shut down his computer, and wondered what in the world he was going to do now. Eventually he picked up a "National Geographic" magazine that was all about the Lewis and Clark Expedition. It was also a guide to the modern trail giving highway numbers and what could be seen. He made a note to discuss this with Sally as a possible vacation/work trip.

Trying to ignore the Lewis and Clark journals was like trying to ignore the "musquetors" that buzzed around the adventurers' heads. His thoughts were just too numerous to dismiss. So, he switched on the computer again and continued.

Chapter 9

Roy worked until past ten in the morning. He had hardly had a chance to even say "good morning" to Sally, as he had his nose in at least three books at a time. Sally understood, he said to himself. "After all, we've been married almost a quarter of a century, and she knew my habits, rude as they are sometimes."

Back his nose went in his books. The only sound to be heard was the soft clicking of his keyboard.

July 25, 1805, Thursday

We got to the three forks of the Missouri River. The north fork seems to be the safest route as it is the widest and least turbulent. We found great quantities of red currents as well as black, purple, and yellow. The cliffs yielded mountain currents, both red and yellow, that have a pine-ish, sweet taste. Choke cherries, boin roche, and red berries are also plentiful.

July 28, 1805, Sunday

According to Sacajawea, exactly where we are camping is the place the Snake Indians were camping five years ago when a band of Minnetares from the Knife River found them. The Snake tribe retreated into the woods hoping to hide from them. However, the Minnetares found them, killed 8 men and women and a number of boys. The rest were taken prisoners. Trying to escape from them, Sacajawea was taken in the middle of the river. I am amazed that she shows no joy at being back in her native country.

August 2, 1805, Friday

We continued our route, but because of the rapids, there was little progress. To my delight, we spotted a lot of wildlife. There were a kind of burrowing squirrel, mallard ducks and red-headed fishing duck, black woodpeckers, several beaver dams with their inhabitants, geese, and rattlesnakes. We passed a small creek on the starboard side that we named Birth Creek in honor of Capt. Clark's birthday.

August 17, 1805, Saturday

Captain Clark, Charbonneau, and Sacajawea, along with me and the others, went out this morning about 7, and it wasn't more than a mile before I saw Sacajawea begin to dance, turning around and pointing to several Indians with joy, and indicating that they are of her tribe. When we arrived, a woman made her way through the crowd and the two embraced. We found that this was Sacajawea's dear friend from childhood, and they had both been taken prisoners in the same battle. Later, when all the greetings and excitement settled down, Sacajawea began to interpret for the captain, but that was interrupted when she jumped up, ran, and embraced a man that turned out to be her brother. She began to weep, and she frequently interrupted her interpretating with her tears. She also learned that all her family was gone except for her two brothers and a nephew.

August 19, 1805, Monday

We connected with a band of Shoshone consisting of about 100 warriors and about three times that many of women and children. In their society, the man is the sole owner of the wives and girl children, and he can dispose of them as he finds proper. Infant daughters are generally sold in marriage to grown men or sons. The girl stays with the parents until they are ready for marriage once they have obtained the age of puberty. Compensation for a daughter given in marriage is generally horses or mules. Women are treated with little respect and are given to all kinds of drudgery whereas the man does little more than hunt and fish.

September 5, 1805, Thursday

We have been with a very strange tribe that has the oddest language we have yet encountered. We can communicate with them only by passing our English through a number of interpreters until they replied and send such through the interpreters again to us. It is slow, but we are getting our needs across to them. They seem to speak with a brogue, and we may have met with the mythical tribe that originated in Wales about 300 years ago. They seem to be friendly and very honest. Capt. Lewis wrote down everything in their language that might help them to discover their origin.

September 12, 1805, Thursday

It is very bad country passing through hills, steep hollows and fallen timber. It took 8 miles, but we crossed a mountain without water and ended up on the hill side of the creek after coming down a long, steep mountain. Horses and men much fatigued.

September 15, 1805, Sunday

We made our way down the right side of the Kos Kos Kee River going over steep points, rocks, and bushes for 4 miles. Several horses slipped and rolled down the steep hills leaving them badly hurt. Two of our horses gave out, but nothing was killed. From this mountain top, I could see high rugged mountains 360° around, and as far as I could see.

October 5, 1805, Saturday

All 38 of our horses were branded and given over to the Nez Percés to care for until our return as the way ahead will be traversed by water.

Capt. Clark is not well with a pain in his gut, but he still is obliged to attend everything. I'm afraid whoever did the cooking added mushrooms to the stew. I told everyone who cooks not to use mushrooms as even the most familiar-looking kind are probably poisonous. I'm hoping nothing like that has happened as that will mean more men sick.

We put our newly built canoes into the water, loaded and tied them off as best we could, and set out.

October 16, 1805, Wednesday

From the first of this journey, I always thought of the Columbia River one of the great objectives of our quest. After all, we were the first white men to see it east of the Cascade Mountains. But things were all business. I do hope when we arrive at the Pacific Ocean, there will be more of a celebration. We have been trying to avoid rapids for obvious reasons. After 14 miles, we encountered a rather bad rapid and decided to portage for almost a mile. We kept on going about 7 miles to the junction of the Snake River and the Columbia. We saw Indians lining the banks. Capt. Clark smoked with their chiefs and gave them tobacco, medals, and shirts. This was gladly accepted, and the tribe became our friends.

October 19, 1805, Saturday

The tribe we encountered near the mouth of the Umatilla River found us to be terrifying. They said we were from the clouds and not men at all. Some wept in our presence and others hid. We gave them little tokens we carried with us and Capt. Clark smoked with the men. Things turned a bit, and the fright went out of them. When Sacajawea came into their camp, circumstances changed even more for the better.

They knew that we had friendly intentions as no war tribe would bring a woman with them.

October 25, 1805, Friday

We need some rest and repair time for our canoes. We've been through some very nasty rapids in the past few days. Even some of the natives are amazed that we made it through.

While the others are busy with the canoes, drying fish, and hunting, I am busy with what I was meant to do on this trip. I have found a whole new world of wildlife here in the northwest. I am seeing birds of all kinds that are not seen in Missouri, along with beaver, frogs, beetles, butterflies, owls, hawks, and a multiplicity of slugs and bugs. My job is to categorize them, describe and sketch them, and how to tell them from Missouri animals. I would love to have one of those lovely birds or magnificent hawks named for me (as I was the first to describe them), but that is not my job. They would be named for me if the people who come after me think I should deserve that. Maybe, if I can come back in 50 years, I'll see Starks Wren, Starks Horned Owl, Starks Purple Butterfly and so forth. I shouldn't be so puffed up as to even think that way.

I have reams and reams of paper that are full of drawings of the local inhabitants, notes of color and size, what category, where they live, etc. that I hope will make it all right back to President Jefferson. With all the canoes that tip over or sink, it's only pure luck sometimes that makes the difference. My next project is the hundreds of varieties of plant life, then insects, and finally I will make a stab at different rocks. Although I'm not trained in geology, I can get local help by leaning on Sacajawea's talents.

October 30, 1805, Wednesday

I have been neglectful in writing in my journal just because I am so busy with my sketches, etc., so I am going to take a piece out of Capt. Clark's journal. (Please keep in mind that the grammar and spelling are his.)

"The day proved cloudy dark and disagreeable with some rain all day which kept us wet. The country a high mountain on each side thickly covered with timber, such as Spruce, Pine, cedar, Oake Cotton &c. &c. I took two men and walked down three miles to examine the Shute [the beginnings of the treacherous rapids called the Cascades] and river below proceeded along an old Indian path, passed. An old village at 1 mile on an elevated Situation, Capt. L. Saw one gun and Several articles which must have been precured from the white people. A wet disagreeable evening, the only wood we could get to burn on this little Island on which we have encamped is the newly discovered [by me] Ash, which makes a tolerable fire."

November 2, 1805, Saturday

In the lower half of the Cascades, and the rapids that have been so numerous and quite dangerous, are now starting to thin out, but not before another rapid proved to be dangerous. Capt. Clark walked the portage, and I walked with him. With all the new species of trees, birds, waterfowl and now even insects, I am busy every moment with sketching and describing these new categories. Capt. Clark is a good companion for this job as he is the first to point out the new species of ash and alder, and unusual waterfowl such as swans, geese, brants, and multiple kinds of ducks, gulls, and plovers.

We camped under a high, projecting rock on the lee side where the mountains leave the river. According to one of the men, this is the place where the river leaves the Cascades behind on the gorge of the Columbia. We are experiencing an ebb tide where the river rose 9 inches which means we are closer to the Pacific than ever.

November 5, 1805, Tuesday

It rained all day, and we were all cold, wet and disagreeable. However, this is the first night we have had no Indians in camp since our arrival on the Columbia which is a blessing as we found the locals to be thievish.

November 7, 1805, Thursday

Capt. Clark wrote:

"Great joy in the camp we are in view of the Ocian, this great Pacific Octean which we been so long anxious to See.   and the roreing or noise made by the waves brakeing on the rockey Shores may be heard."

Capt. Clark was wrong: we camped at Pillar Rock tonight, and I know, from my study of the maps, that the ocean cannot be seen from there. He is just so anxious to see the Pacific that he made this error.

November 15, 1805, Friday

The ocean is immediately in front and gives us, and from that we can see Cape Disappointment to Point Addams. I am in the upper part of Haleys Bay.

December 25, 1805, Wednesday, Christmas Day

After days and days of rain, we finally come to the joyous occasion of Christmas. Songs were sung which all joined in gladly. Our tobacco was divided among our smokers, and those that did not indulge were given handkerchiefs. Despite all the merriment we tried to generate, it kept raining making things rather disagreeable.   Even the dinner was poor: spoiled elk, pounded fish, also spoiled, and a few roots.

January 6, 1806, Monday

Capt. Clark, after an early breakfast, set out with 2 canoes and 12 men in search of a whale. Included in the party were Charbonneau and his wife Sacajawea. After traveling with the expedition for a long time to see the great waters and the monstrous fish that lived there, we came across the skeleton of an enormous whale that we measured at 105 feet.

January 9, 1806, Thursday

Because the Indians informed us that the people who visit the entrance to this river speak the same language as ourselves, I believe them to be either English or American. They even repeated what they had learned from these visitors, words such as musket, powder, shot, knife, file, damned rascal, son of a bitch, &c.

January 29, 1806, Wednesday

In Captain Lewis's words, "Nothing worthy of notice occurred today." And that's the way it's been since we landed at Ft. Clatsop. There is really nothing to do, discover, divert or entertain us at all. I, personally, have been rather busy with the discoveries of new plants and trees. The descriptions of these plants are fully covered in my botanical notes along with the sketches and descriptions.

February 15, 1806, Saturday

On a day when Capt. Lewis was obviously bored and was making lists for some reason, he wrote the following:

"The quadrupeds of this country from the Rocky Mountains to the pacific Ocean are 1st the domestic animals, consisting or the horse and the dog only; 2edly the native wild animals, consisting of the Brown white of grizly bear, (which I believe to be the same family with a mearly accidental difference in point of colour) the black bear, the common red deer, the black tailed fallow deer, the Mule deer, Elk, the large brown wolf, the small woolf of the plains, the large wolf of the plains, the tiger car, the common red fox, black fox or fisher, silver fox, large red fox of the plains, small fox of the plains or kit fox, Antelope, sheep, beaver, common otter, sea Otter, mink, spuck, seal, racoon, large grey squirrel, small brown squirrel, small grey squirrel, ground squirrel, sewelet, Braro, rat, mouse, mole, Panther, hare, rabbit and polecat or skunk."

This may be interesting to someone, but this is all posted in great detail along with sketches in my animal reports.

February 20, 1806, Thursday

We were visited by a Chief of the Chinooks with 25 of his men. He and his companions were friendly, and we gave them something to eat and lots of smoke. The chief got a small medal which he seemed to like. At sunset, we asked that they leave as is our custom and closed our gates. No matter how friendly they seem, we are very wary of their motives and do not allow overnight guests.

March 20, 1806, Thursday

Rain has continued along with violent winds, and that has delayed our departure for home. I'm sure that I have changed, matured, and will be looking forward to being again with my family. And never more have to eat elk!

March 23, 1806, Sunday

After our landmark mission to the Northwest, the Lewis and Clark expedition turned around and headed for home.

April 1, 1806, Tuesday

When we finally were able to push off and make for home, the rain was so incessant that we had to hug the shore in order to get anywhere. We were met by several canoes of

Indians, mostly women and children, who were in search of food. Their stores of dried fish had run out, and the spring run had not yet started and probably wouldn't for a month.

Capt. Lewis purchased a canoe from an Indian for which he paid 6 fathoms of wampum beads. The Indian got in another canoe and departed seemingly satisfied with the beads. However, he soon returned and gave back the beads and took the canoe. This method of trading is considered fair by them.

April 6, 1806, Sunday

142 miles up the Columbia River is the entrance into the Pacific Ocean. I hope this will be the final start home. We had dried meat that was loaded into the canoes. We passed an encampment we had on November 3rd, and I could judge from what the water was then is now about 12 feet higher. The rain has been continuous with high winds and often impedes our progress.

April 9, 1806, Wednesday

We proceeded to the Wah-chel-lah village where one of our men spotted the tomahawk that was stolen from Capt. Clark back in November. So, naturally the captain took it, but he had to wrest it away from locals saying that it was purchased. It was settled by neighbors who said it was indeed stolen.

We passed through the lowest rapid at the foot of the Cascades and entered the Gorge of the Columbia.

April 12, 1806, Saturday

I observed that the mountains are covered with fir of several species and the white cedar. We also see cottonwood, sweet willow, maple, a broad leaf ash, the purple haw, a type of cherry, purple currant, gooseberry, red willow, vining and whiteberry, honeysuckle, sacacommis, and 2 species of mountain holly.

Because of the disagreeable weather, we are wet, miserable and impeded. We have only gone 7 miles in the last 3 days.

April 24, 1806, Thursday

With the almost impossible travel by canoe, we have decided to make the rest of the journey by land. We came across several tribes that we tried to bargain with for horses and other necessities, and many of them turned out to be nothing but thieves. Some of our goods, including goods for horses, we traded in good faith only to have them "missing" soon after. We recovered some of them, and Capt. Clark brandished his gun and said that he would shoot any Indian who tried to take anything that did not belong to them and even burn their houses. Our goods were confined, and horses hobbled in our coral under strict guard. With these things intact, we were able to travel 12 miles today.

April 30, 1806, Wednesday

We have found the Walla Walla tribe to be very welcoming and willing to please. While there, Capt. Clark's white horse, that was given to him by the great Chief Yellepit, went missing, and all the men went looking for it, but came back empty-handed. When informed about the horse, the Chopunnish man took Capt. Lewis's horse and went looking. Within half an hour he returned with it. By 11 in the morning, we had departed from those honest, friendly Walla Walla people accompanied by our guide and Chopunnish man and family.

May 10, 1806, Saturday

We had wind from the S.W. along with rain most of yesterday. By 9 P.M. it turned to snow and kept up all night. So, this morning we had 8 inches of snow on the ground, but we proceeded through the open plain. The horses tripped often on the slippery ground and clogged snow.

September 20, 1806, Saturday

Today marks the "almost" end of our journey. A shout of joy was given when we realized that we had just entered a French village called La Charette, the first white village we have seen since we left. We asked permission and received it to fire off our guns in joy. Three rounds and a hearty cheer!

May 30, 1806, Friday

One of the men brought me an interesting species of onion from below the Falls of Columbia. Although each was about the size of a nutmeg, they grew together in doubles. The leaves were flat and solid. The taste was the crispiest and the most delicately flavored I had ever tried, more sweet than pungent. I hope I come across them again.

One of our canoes, after being loaded with trade goods, landed on the opposite shore, and was caught in a nasty current. It filled with water and sunk right away. One of the men in the canoe was not a swimmer and barely made it to shore. Clothing was one of the items lost and given the scant state of our attire these days, that was a concerning loss.

June 6, 1806, Sunday

Below the Great Rapids of Columbia, we were visited by about 12 Indians, one being the chief of the Clahclahlah's nation. We did some horse trading, mainly to get animals that would make it over the Rocky Mountains. After the trading was done, the men and Indians had foot races and played prisoner's base until midnight. We were all in good humor when the chief announced that we would be unable to cross the Mountains until the next full moon, about July 1st. This was disagreeable with us. After much discussion, we considered everything, and a time was set that most of the Indians deemed most proper, the middle of this month.

June 10, 1806, Tuesday

We packed up and left about 11 o'clock feeling the time was right and ourselves equipped and ready for the trip over the Rockies. The hills were extremely high and about three miles in extent. The pass over Collins Creek was deeply muddy and very difficult, but we made it.

The country we passed through is very fertile and almost stone-free. The land is well-packed with species of fir, long leafed pine, and larch. Choke cherry is in the undergrowth along with black alder, two species of shoemate, purple haw, service berry, goose berry, wild rose, honeysuckle, and a species of dwarf pine. This whole trip has been a botanist's dream!

June 17, 1806, Tuesday

We find that we are at the mercy of the mountains, and things look bleak. There is anywhere from 8 to 12 feet of snow, even on the south side, and, as a consequence, our horses have no food. There is also a lack of food for us. Numerous people have gone out hunting and have come back with nothing.

Since we have a choice, we have decided to turn back. If we don't, we'll probably become stranded in the mountains without any provisions. Going back to our last encampment would mean we could somehow get or hire an Indian guide from among the Shoshone to get us over the mountains.

Capt. Clark thought it would hasten things if we left some of our baggage there. Many of his papers were wrapped and protected from the elements. I thought they would be safe, but we were not at all sure that we would be coming back the same way, therefore losing valuable papers and supplies.

June 26, 2806, Thursday

We set out early this morning down Hungary Creek. When we got to the summit, it was where we had left our extra baggage and Capt. Clark's papers. I was quite relieved.

June 29, 1806, Sunday

We descended to and passed the main branch of the Kooskooke just above the entrance of Glade Creek where we said a fond farewell to the snow. We found plenty of grass waiting for our horses. We stopped for a meal after a 12-mile journey, and afterwards 7 miles more that brought us over to Lolo Pass, the last divide of the Bitterroot Mountains and down to Lolo Creek.

August 6, 1806, Wednesday

I found that July was a duplicate of the time we spent leaving St. Louis 2½ years ago. Nothing of any consequence happened on this part of the journey. The hunting was good, and one man brought back a swan-like bird that I couldn't identify. I'll have to add that to my endless list of unknown species that I will deal with in St. Louis when I meet with local experts. They may not know any more than I do about this list and sketches.

August 11, 1806, Monday

Since I had decided to follow Capt. Lewis on his alternate journey, and I accidentally left my journal in the pack with Capt. Clark, I have been without records of these days. Capt. Lewis asked me the other day why I wasn't writing a

journal anymore; I explained to him what had happened. He generously shared a blank journal with me so I wouldn't miss any more records of the journey. He said he would share his journal with me to fill in the missing time when we got back to St. Louis.

A herd of elk was spotted on a thick willow bar, Capt. Lewis, who was determined to kill some, and went off with Cruzatte. He told us later that he had been shot in the left thigh that had gone through the hinder area and the ball traveled through the right side. At first, he thought it was Cruzatte that had accidently shot him, but when he couldn't find him no matter how much hallooing he shouted, he assumed it was Indians. He got back to camp as quickly as possible and had everyone on the alert. Capt. Lewis sent off a party to look for the Indians, but they came back after not seeing any. So, the blame fell on Curzatte again when they got the ball that shot me and found it a spot match for his.

We finally met up with Capt. Clark and his party, and I'm happy to say they are all well. Needless to say, Capt. Lewis's condition is extremely painful, and he will now let his friend, Capt. Clark, continue their journal.

September 23, 1806, Tuesday

About 12 o'clock, we arrived at the Mississippi after descending from the river that started out our journey 2½ years ago in St. Charles. The inhabitants were warm and welcoming, giving us a fine dinner, and we fired off our pieces in salute to the town.

I visited my parents as soon as I had a minute. Mother, being who she is, saw me and cried. Dad gave me a hug and slapped me on the back. They both wanted to know so much about the expedition, and they asked so many questions that I had to tell them that I would bring in my journal for them to read. It was so good to see them again!

Capt. Lewis had us unloading the canoes and storing our goods. I told them how much it had meant to me to be able to be a part of this expedition, and I wanted to go to the university and get a degree in biology. Nothing, however, could have taught me more than what I learned with Captains Clark and Lewis. Everyone was surprised that we only lost one man on the journey, and that was Sgt. Charlies Floyd, and he died of a burst appendix. I will miss these men on whom I learned so much of companionship and working tightly together. I hope all their lives go on as well as I envision for my own.

* * * * * *

Roy sighed. He felt like he had lost a good friend now that Johnny's story had been told. He understood that it was long, but it was so exciting that he had to include as much as he could. He hoped his editor wouldn't cut too much of it.

Johnny had seemed like a mirror of himself when he was that age. In a way. But that's what happens: so many writer's characters reflect themselves. Like Johnny, when he finished high school, he wanted to get right into it and write the "great American novel." He found that the publishing business was hard, and others blocked his way. So, after several years of trying, he capitulated and went to college. But that time off taught him many things, multiple lessons that helped him survive. Like Johnny.

At the university, he wrote his first novel during his junior year and received nothing but praise from his professors. That's all he needed, just a little interest. Now he was the author of 12 novels, all hits except his fifth, "Chicago Wayward." Every time he thought of it, he mentally kicked himself and asked why he had bothered with that book. Sally never brought it up like she did his other novels, and when she did, she treaded very lightly.

There were times, though, that when he thought of Johnny, he always wanted to throw up his arms and yell! He was so elated that he had paved Johnny's way to the university with an experience not unlike his. He would always think of Johnny kindly, as a buddy, even as a father to him.

Chapter 10

A few nights later at dinner, Roy broached a subject so startling that Sally could only stare at him with a forkful of chicken parmesan halfway to her mouth.

"How about we take a vacation and follow the trail of Lewis and Clark," he said in a completely off-handed manner.

The forkful of dinner clattered back onto her plate.

"Now why in the name of Paul Bunyan would you want to do that! Didn't you have enough of that in you last month of writing a journal for Johnny? I have a better idea. Let's follow the trail of the Donner Party in winter and end up eating each other."

"Yeah, well..."

"You just got too wrapped up in the story yourself, and you need to let go," she said kindly.

"I just wanted to see what you would think of such an idea."

"Why on earth would you even come near such a subject when you know my asthma keeps me indoors most of the time."

Roy smiled slightly. "Well, if you could, would you?"

"I never even considered it. I left hiking and the wilderness behind after my first attack. I won't say that I don't miss it, because I do, but it's totally unrealistic. Please, let's talk about something else."

"Okay, but what you said about the Donner Party, it gave me an instant idea. I could write about that since one of my ancestors was part of that, I'm sad to say. I believe only he and his daughter survived."

"My, you do have a wide range of situations for your relatives, don't you?"

"And it's the first one in this series that I know for sure existed."

Sally stared at him. "What branch did he or she come from?"

"I believe it was one that came from England. Carson was the name, I think. Is that English or maybe Swedish?" he inquired.

"Don't know, but what a tangled mess that wagon train went through."

"I'm going to have to look into that. It could be something I could use. I wonder if old Carson kept a journal. Wouldn't that be a prize to discover! I think I'll get a hold of my third cousin, Mazie, the one in San Bernardino."

"How in the heck do you know all these people, and how do you keep in touch?" Sally asked with a flabbergasted tone in her voice.

"Come into my office after dinner, and I'll show you my charts. It's not hard keeping up with the family if you have communications. Mazie happens to be the only third cousin that I keep in touch with. I know she has brothers, but I haven't charted them yet. The Carsons almost disappeared in the Sierra Nevadas, but Lorna, only eight at the time, got lucky that she and her father were rescued."

"Oh, I just must read this one. Get going on it."

"I'll have to put in a ton of research before I can even start," Rob reminded her.

"Should we go to the library or rely on the computer?"

"I'm probably have to mark up the books, so best I go to Amazon for that."

94

"Good thinking." That being said, she resumed her meal.

Roy spent the next day going through his internet for information and was richly rewarded with many books and research notes. The materials arrived in the next two days, and he immersed himself in the six books he found online. Once read, he felt confident enough to start writing.

* * * * *

April 8, 1846

"I heard something from Lawson Smith that we should look into right away," Len

Carson said as he rushed into the house. His wife, Minnie, paused what she was doing and listened.

"You know how we're always talking about going to California?"

Minnie nodded, her face brightening.

"George Donner and his brother, Jacob, are getting a wagon train together, and leaving for Independence, Missouri, you know, where the Oregon Trail begins. If we want to see California in our lifetimes, now is the time to act. You willing?"

"How much time to we have?"

"Not much. Donner has this timed for when the rains end and there's grass for the oxen to eat. He wants to get there before the snow makes the Sierra Nevada impassable. So, it's now or never, my love. Let's take it. The kids will love it!"

"I have so much to do to get things together," versing her thoughts. "I don't know how much time I'll need. Let's get that trunk down from the attic. I can probably get Lorna and

Lennie's things in that and maybe some of mine. We'll have to leave so much behind, like my mother's furniture."

"We can sell that."

"Is there time?"

"I'm sure someone will be delighted to have it, and we'll have money for the trip.

I think I'll go over to the Donner place and talk to George about it. He lives on the other side of Springfield, so I'll be gone for a while. I'll help you with the trunk first. After I see George, I'll go to Lawson's house to see if he was serious about selling his oxen to me. That's what we'll need to pull that wagon of ours."

It was a two hundred fifty-mile trip from Springfield, Illinois to Independence, Missouri, and Donner was anxious to get going. Len wanted to leave within the next five to six days. He knew he had to hurry with his preparations, while Minnie was frantic to get all the things done before stepping off into the unknown.

But, somehow, they got the most important things done: clothing and food packed, the yoke of oxen procured, the furniture sold and, somehow, they were able to get everything in the wagon. They even brought one of their beds for the children to sleep in. Minnie would sleep on the floor of the wagon, and Len would sleep under it. So, when the Donner party came by, they were ready to join them.

Day 1 – April 15, 1846

Len and Minnie waited anxiously at the front of their house, and the kids were bouncing up and down on the one bed they were taking. It seemed to be the only way to handle their anxious energy.

It was a small house they were leaving, but Minnie loved it. It was the only one they had ever owned together. Her kitchen was the front of the fireplace and the table, and fixing dinner could be a challenge, but Minnie didn't really mind. She was in the middle of teaching Lorna how to cook on the fireplace, and that knowledge would become useful once they were on their way. It would be great to have a helper out on the open prairie.

Suddenly, far away, they could hear a clumsy rumbling. With that kind of sound, it could only be a group of wagons. Lorna and Lennie stopped jumping and peeked out from behind their mother.

"Look!" Lorna almost screamed, "they have three wagons for one family." Puzzled, she turned to her father and asked, "How come they have three and we only have one?"

"Seems like they're taking all their furniture as well as food and clothing. And, besides, they're the leaders and probably need more equipment."

Just at that moment, James Reed's three wagons came into sight.

"Don't even ask," Len said to his daughter.

Len slipped down off the wagon seat and went to greet the families and introduce his bunch to the others.

"Good to have you with us, Len," James said with a robust handshake. "And I see you have two kids with you," he said pointing to Lorna and Lennie who quickly dropped out of eyesight. "Can't have them too shy out on the prairie and through the mountains. Gotta speak up and not be afraid of anything."

"There's nothing wrong with those kids that a little familiarity won't cure," Len explained.

"What say we get going?" George Donner asked firmly. "It's a long way to Missouri, and we must meet up with another train there. Don't want to keep them waiting, ya know."

Before Len could slap the oxen into moving, Minnie took one last look at her house. The kids behind her began waving goodbye to the structure.

Day 25

The small train arrived at Independence, Missouri, and spent the next few the next few days outfitting their rigs with the final touches.

Day 33

About 100 miles west of Independence was Indian Creek where the Donner party caught up with a longer wagon train led by Col. William Russell.

Day 41

In what is now Kansas, the Russell train was stopped at the Big Blue River due to high water. To get their wagons across, rafts were built.

Day 43

James Reed's mother-in-law, Sarah Keyes, died while the train was camped. They buried her under a tree near Alcove Springs. She was the first death the train experienced, and she was the only one to die from old age.

Day 63

George Donner's wife, Tamsen, wrote in her journal that they were now at the Platt River, about 200 miles from Fort Laramie in what is now Wyoming. She noted that the trip had been better than expected. So far. And so far as the Carson wagon was traveling, everything was very satisfactory: the kids were rambunctious and into everything, however, Lorna was getting better and better at cooking. Lennie had firewood duty; loved the freedom that came with it, but he had also been warned sternly that danger lurks not far from the wagon train, and he had to keep his head on straight.

Day 65

Head of the wagon train, William Russell resigned as he and others had decided to travel ahead to Fort Laramie to trade in their wagons and oxen for mules because they were faster.

Day 74

The Donner Party arrived at Fort Laramie where James Reed met an old mountaineer, James Clyman. Clyman just came by horse from California via a new route. Called the Hastings Cutoff, he warned the emigrants not to take it, but to go the regular route. He claimed it was too dangerous and difficult, especially for wagons.

Day 80

The party celebrated the Fourth of July at Fort Laramie. The fireworks were a special treat for Lennie, but Lorna plugged her ears and went to the wagon.

Day 93

The Donner party and a lone eastbound rider met at Independence Rock that handed them an open letter from Hastings asking that all emigrants on the road should meet him at Fort Bridger, so he can guide them on his cutoff.

Day 94

This was the halfway point for the expedition. They had crossed the Continental Divide and traveled 1,000 miles but still had 1,000 more to go. Although a small victory, it was still a reason for the little family to celebrate.

Day 95

At Little Sandy Creek, the train met with several other trains. "Here is where decisions are made," Len said to his family. "Here we decide to make the choice of going onto the Hastings Cutoff which is said to take 350 to 400 miles off the journey, or to stick to the tried-and-true way of getting to California."

"What are we going to do, Pa?" Lorna asked.

"Well, I think we should vote on it. We can stay with Mr. Donner and go with his choice, the Hastings Cutoff, or we can go with the other group. What do you think we ought to do?"

"If it means less time on the road, I say stay with Mr. Donner," Len voted.

"But," Lorna countered, "we've had warnings about the Cutoff. It's not the best way to go. We need to be sure and go with the other group."

"You're just chicken," Lennie taunted.

Before Lorna could counter, Len spoke up. "These are very good reasons on both sides. It seems that Ma and I have the deciding votes. My vote is to go with the Hastings cutoff. It may be a little rougher, but it's shorter. What about you, Ma?"

She looked unsure but voted with Len.

"Okay, it looks like it's the Cutoff for us. I'll go tell Mr. Donner."

And so, the next day they took the left-hand cutoff toward Fort Bridger with those of the Donner Party.

Day 103

Consisting of a corral and two cabins, Fort Bridger, of mountaineer Jim Bridger fame, became the Donner Party's haven for the next four days, days to make repairs and rest the oxen. There they learned that Hastings had left the previous week, but he left instructions for later groups to follow him.

Day 107

Fort Bridger, the Donner party took on some new members that brought up their number to seventy-four people. According to James Reed, he wrote, "Hastings Cutoff is said to be a saving of 350 or 400 miles and a better route. The rest of the Californians went the long route, feeling afraid of Hastings' cutoff. But Mr. Bridger informs me that it is a fine, level road with plenty of water and grass. It is estimated that 700 miles will take us to Captain Sutter's fort, which we hope to make in seven weeks from this day." With that, the Donner Party left Fort Bridger on the Hastings Cutoff.

Day 113

Near the mouth of Echo Canyon on the Weber River, the Donner Party stopped. Hastings has left a note for them that the road ahead is impassable and they need to send someone ahead to get instructions. Following the wagon tracks of Hastings group, James Reed and two others made the trip.

Day 117

James Reed returned to the wagons. He blazed a rough trail from where Hastings pointed out an alternative route.

Day 118

In the Wasatch Mountains, the Donner Party was slowed down due to the necessity of chopping a road through the brush and trees. The slowdown allowed the Graves Family to catch up with the train bringing the number of travelers to 87 in 23 wagons.

Day 129

Having departed the Weber River using East Canyon, the Donner Party entered the Salt Lake Valley. With 600 miles left to go, there was only a month of summer left.

Day 132

Tuberculosis claimed the life of Luke Halloran and was buried in a coffin at a fork in the road. Then another note from Hastings warned them of a two-day drive across the Salt Lake Valley where there is no water, but they continued to follow the tracks of the Hastings Party.

"Pa, I'm thirsty," Lennie said.

"You know where the water is. Go get a drink," Len said.

"I'm not really thirsty, I just think about the trip across the desert, and I think thirsty."

Len's hearty laugh echoed across the canyon.

Day 137

Before the dry drive began, the Party reached Redlum Spring, the last source of water. After filling up with as much water as they could hold, they set out to cross the Great Salt Lake Desert.

Day 141

It was only the third day, but the water ran out. During the night, the Reed's thirsty oxen ran off, gone for good. The Reeds set out on foot carrying a few possessions.

Day 146

It took five days and eighty miles to cross that desert, twice what Hastings had reported. In that time, they lost thirty-six head of cattle and four wagons that had to be abandoned. Hunting for cattle, recuperating from their ordeal, and facing the possibility of carrying their possessions were the main activities.

Day 148

After taking inventory, the Donner Party realized that it didn't have enough food for the trip to California. To request more, Charles Stanton and William McCutchen were sent on ahead to Sutter's Fort.

Day 164

At the Humboldt River where the Cutoff meets the traditional trail, the Party learned that the traditional trail was 125 miles shorter than the Cutoff. Two Native Americans joined the party temporarily.

Day 173

A fight broke out between Reed's teamster, Milt Elliott and the driver of Graves' wagon, John Snyder, when their teams become entangled while trying to get up a sandy hill. When Reed got in the middle to separate the teams using a knife, Snyder hit Reed on the head with his whip handle. Reed could see that Snyder was about to come at him again, so he stabbed him in the chest. Snyder collapsed and died after floundering up the sandy hill. For that, some wanted Reed to hang, but he ended up banished from the wagon train.

Day 175

Reed, who was heading west, overtook the Donners who had gone ahead of the rest of the train. Realizing that time was short, the party traveled as quickly as possible while going along the Humbolt River.

Ma, why are we going so fast? Won't that just wear out the team faster?" Lorna asked.

"Yes, I guess it will, but we must move on faster. That's one of the reasons we're walking. If we lighten the load, then it's easier for the oxen to pull the wagon. It's October already, you know, and in the mountains, we'll get snow sooner and heavier than we would on the flatlands."

"I don't understand why, Ma. Aren't the mountains on the same area as the flatlands?" Lennie whined.

"You must understand that the higher you go, the colder it is, and that means snow sooner. And plenty of it! We don't want to be caught in the mountains with so much snow that we can't move. Where would we get food? Where would we find shelter?"

Lennie's brow furrowed for a minute. "I understand," he said quietly.

"Look, Ma, isn't that Mr. Hardkoop sitting by the side of the road?" Lorna pointed out.

"I wonder why that dear old man is not walking. You two keep walking, I'm going to find out what's going on."

She was gone for only a few minutes.

"What did you find out, Ma?" Lorna asked.

"He couldn't keep up with the train, but no one can take him. I don't know what is going to happen to him."

And that's the last they saw of the old man: sitting down by the road, hugging his knees, head hanging.

Day 179

Twenty-one of the train's oxen were killed and eighteen were stolen by Paiute Indians. More than 100 of the party's oxen were now gone.

104

Day 181

A man named Wolfinger stopped at the Humbolt Sink to cache his wagon considering the Indian raids that have killed most of his cattle. Two men stayed with him to help, but they returned without him saying that Indians had killed him. One of those men later confessed to killing Wolfinger.

Day 184

The Truckee River, the landmark that would lead them into the Sierra Nevada, was finally reached by the Donner Party.

Day 193

When Charles Stanton returned from Sutter's Fort, he brought seven mules that were loaded with provisions, a saving grace since the emigrants' food was almost gone. He also brought Luis and Salvadore, two newly baptized Native American guides. There is also news: the pass that goes through the Sierras should be open for another month.

Day 199

While making a new front axle for his wagon, George Donner cut his hand badly. As the rest of the party moved on, George and Jacob's group loitered behind.

Day 200

As fast as the declining oxen could haul the almost-empty wagons, they pushed on until, near Truckee Lake, they reached the foot of the main ridge. Although the weather was clear, there was a ring around the moon announcing a coming storm.

Day 201

The party tried to make it over the pass, but the promised storm had brought five feet of snow. Too exhausted to push on, they huddled together against a storm of snow and sleet that night. The next day they returned to the eastern end of the lake. Only 150 miles from Sutter's Fort, the group has traveled 2,500 miles. Bringing up the rear, the Donners are still held up by the accident.

Day 219

The Donner Party camped for the winter. There were abandoned cabins, others are constructed along with lean-tos, and the Donner families erected tents, and the single men built a brush shelter.

Day 220

Most of the cattle had been slaughtered for food.

Day 221

Twenty-two members started across the mountains by foot but returned two days later after an unsuccessful attempt.

Day 236

After days of snow and sleet, it finally let up. Graves and Stanton wanted to make another try at crossing the mountains, so they decided to make snowshoes out of rawhide and oxbows. For everyone, it was hard to find wood.

Day 239

Patrick Breen's family took in Mr. Spitzer who was so weak from starvation that he needed help just to stand up. Mr. Stanton started begging for beef for his Indians and himself.

Day 243

Using the home-made snowshoes, Stanton and Graves and some others planned to cross the mountain and were preparing.

Day 246

The band of emigrants on snowshoes began to cross the mountains. The seventeen consisted of five young women, nine men and twelve-year-old Lemuel Murphy. Each carried six days of starvation rations, a rifle, a blanket, a hatchet, and a pistol. Their goal was Bear Valley

Day 247

Two of the snowshoers found that they couldn't keep up and returned to camp.

Day 248

Those on snowshoes got over the summit.

Day 250

The snowshoers reached a place called Yuba Bottoms.

Day 251

Stanton, who had been straggling for several days, said he would catch up later, and he stopped to rest. His remains were found there a year later. Back in camp, Sam Shoemaker, Rinehart, and Smith also died.

Day 254

Christmas Eve. The snowshoers had been out of rations for three days, and they had become confused and lost in the mountains. It was suggested by Patrick Dolan that one person should volunteer to die to save the rest. They decided that they would wait until the first one fell. Animal handler and Mexican teamster, Antonio, was first, and not much longer was Franklin Graves.

Day 255

Christmas Day. Margaret Reed had hidden away enough food to make a pot of soup for her children, but by January they were starving. She considered eating the ox hides that made up her roof. With no other choice, she sacrificed the roof, but it made their cabin uninhabitable, so they moved in with the Breens. In the snowshoe camp, Patrick Dolan and young Lemuel Murphy died.

Day 256

Without looking at each other and crying, the snowshoers resorted to cannibalism.

Day 260

When the human flesh ran out, some of the snowshoers discussed killing the two Native Americans, Salvatore, and Luis. William Eddy told the Indians, and they quietly vanished into the woods.

Day 268

With Lennie's body cuddled in her arms, Minnie Carson died of starvation.

"Pa, we're alone now," Lorna bravely reminded her father. "I can take care of you. Ma taught me lots of things."

"I'm sure you can," Len said wiping his eyes. "We have to hang on for each other so we can tell everyone what went on here."

"What do you mean, Pa? Everyone seems so hushed about something. What is everyone hiding? You can tell me. I'm a big girl. I'm nine now."

"You are right. Sit down and I'll tell you the ugly truth and we can thank God that we weren't a part of it."

Day 270

What emigrants were left of the snowshoers came across Luis and Salvadore who hadn't eaten for nine days. They were on the brink of death and William Foster shot them, thinking this was the only way to avoid imminent death by starvation.

Day 278

The snowshoers reached an Indian village. Startled at first by the emigrant's starved appearance, they shared what meager food they had. Foster and the five women who are left were too weak to continue.

Day 279

William Eddy gave an Indian a pouch of tobacco to get him to the next settlement, Johnson's Ranch, which was several miles away. Settlers were taken aback at the emaciated wreck, and they followed his bloody footprints back to the village to bring back the rest of what was left of the party. Of the seventeen people who were members of the snowshoe party, seven had died and two turned back.

Day 295

The proprietor of Sutter's Fort, John Sutter, and the fort's commander, Captain Edward Kern, offered three dollars a day to anyone who would join a rescue party.

Day 297

A rescue party, called the First Relief, that included William Eddy, began the trek from the Sacramento Valley. Although they were delayed by rain and a swollen river, they made steady progress, stowing food at stations along the way so they didn't have to carry it all. Three of the ten turned back, but the rest kept on going.

Day 300

Selim E. Woodworth, a San Francisco naval officer, had been put in charge of recovery operations with James Reed to lead the rescue party called the Second Relief. The two men set out from San Francisco. Woodworth was headed for Sutter's Fort, while Reed intentioned to cross San Francisco Bay to recruit both men and horses in the Sonoma and Napa areas. Back at camp, William Eddy's wife, Eleanor, died.

Day 303

Although all are out of any kind of meat, and their hides are nearly gone, one diarist wrote, "...spring will soon be upon us."

Milt Elliot and Augustus Spitzer died.

Day 304

The First Relief reached a place called Mule Springs, four miles beyond the snowline.

Day 310

After taking eleven days, Woodworth arrived at Sutter's Fort, fighting the Sacramento River's current and the wind. He left the same day for Johnson's Ranch, which was the staging point of the Second Relief.

Day 312

A rescuer recalled, "At sunset, we crossed Truckee Lake on the ice, and came to the spot where, we had been told, we should find the emigrants. We looked all around, but no living thing except ourselves was in sight. We raised a loud hello. And then we saw a woman emerge from a hole in the snow. As we approached her, several others made their appearance. They were gaunt with famine; and I can never forget the horrible ghastly sight they presented. The first woman spoke in a hollow voice, very much agitated, and said, "Are you men from California or do you come from heaven?"'

Day 315

Twenty-three refugees left the camp with the First Relief rescuers. Thirty-three were left to wait for the Second Relief. From the cut he obtained earlier, George Donner's arm was so gangrenous he couldn't move.

"Lorna, we're going to go to California, and this time we'll make it!"

"Isn't it exciting, Pa?"

"I just wish your mother and brother could have seen this day."

But Lorna didn't say a word. In fact, she never spoke about her mother or sibling again. But to her credit, she did her best to take care of her father.

There were thirty-one people still left at the camp since fourteen of them have died.

Day 317

Traveling with the First Relief, John Denton, unable to keep up, had to be left behind.

Day 318

Ada Keseberg died and was buried in the snow. According to Mrs. Murphy, wolves were hovering around her shanty about to dig up the bodies buried around her.

Day 319

Mrs. Murphy said she was hungry enough to eat her husband. No one was sure if she had or hadn't eaten fellow travelers, and most didn't care. The Donners told the California people that if they didn't find their cattle, that were probably under ten to twelve feet of snow, and the Murphy family would start to eat the dead. Others suspected they had already indulged.

Day 321

Heading down the mountain, the First Relief team passed the Second Relief team going up the mountain. James Reed met his wife and two of his children after five months of separation. The other two were still at the camp.

Day 328

The worst storm of the season hit, and the Second Relief and charges were caught at the crest of what is now Donner Pass. Unable to move, they spent two days trying to keep warm on a fire they could barely keep lit. After the storm, most of the emigrants were too weak to move. Three children are taken by Reed and his companions, leaving the rest. In what would become known as "Starved Camp," three died and were cannibalized by the others. Lewis, Jacob Donner's son, died as the storm ended.

Day 334

Arriving at the Lake, Eddy and Foster found that James and George, their sons, have died leaving only nine people alive in the camp.

Day 359

The Fourth Relief party reached the camp and found Lewis Keseberg the only one alive. He said George Donner had died and so had Mrs. Murphy. Tamsen Donner came through on her way over the pass and died that night. The salvage party was suspicious of Keseberg's story as they found a pot of human flesh, George Donner's Pistols, jewelry, and money in gold.

Day 363

With Keseberg in tow, the Fourth Relief left the camp.

Day 371

Lewis Keseberg, the last member of the Donner Party, arrived at Sutter's Fort.

Day 394

Heading east, General Stephen W. Kearny reached the "Cannibal Camp" as he called it. His party gathered whatever remains they could find and put them into the Breen cabin where the bodies were buried and set the cabin on fire.

"Pa, why did all this happen?" asked Lorna thoughtfully.

"God knows. I'm afraid I don't," Len replied.

"What will happen to us now?"

"Oh, we'll get that homestead in California like we planned. Maybe I'll even marry again."

"I don't want you to marry again. I just want it you and I."

"Having a new Ma wouldn't be so bad, now, would it? Just think, I may even be able to give you a new brother or sister."

"Okay, but make it a sister, would you? I think I need a change."

Chapter 11

It was one of Sally's unusual "vacation" days, meaning she had no meetings to go to, the boss was out of the country, and she was caught up on all her paperwork. She thoroughly enjoyed the rarity of the day. That is until Roy came into her line of sight over her newspaper. He was in one of his desperate moods where he couldn't find out anything and expected her to know just what he needed. She sighed and looked up and asked if there was anything she could do.

"How much of Iowa history do you remember?" he asked.

"Not much. Why?"

"Because I have a lead on something, and I can't find anything to back it up."

"What have you been checking in on?"

"The encyclopedia. I'm afraid it's really out-of-date."

"Why is it out of date?" she asked, quite puzzled.

"Because they only list this incident and a tiny bit of information, but it seemed like it could be a lot more. I was hoping you could tell me more about the 'Spirit Lake Massacre'."

Now, Sally understood. "I can tell you why there isn't much about it in an old book. The incident was of a very delicate nature, and how old is your reference?"

"Published in 1947."

"When I was a kid, that sort of thing was not unusual. Because of the delicate nature of the massacre, it was just not published. What does the encyclopedia say about it?"

"It says where it took place at Spirit Lake, what happened, and that's about all."

"Nothing more?"

"No, nothing. What am I going to do to fill in the missing facts?"

"Do what you always do. Keep looking. The library is open until nine tonight. Oh, wait. I think I have something. If I still have it, it will be in the back of my shelves."

Looking hopeful, Roy said with a note of hope in his voice, "I'll sit here and wait until you find it."

"Settle back, get a cup of coffee, and I'll start looking."

Sally left for her bookshelves in the attic right away. It took all of six minutes to find it. She grabbed it and realized she was reinforcing the myth that she had all the answers. Oh, well, so be it.

Holding the book over her head, she slipped it to Roy.

"This should hold you. You want to know about everything that happened, well, you've got it. The book was written in Victorian English by the author who was one of four women captured by the Indians and escaped being murdered. Her name was Abbie Gardner-Sharp. We had to know everything about the massacre because it was Iowa, and the teacher found enough copies for all of us in the class."

"And how long were you living in Iowa?"

"Two years. Do you want the book?"

"Yes, of course. Thank you so much!"

"I'm just glad it ended up being used. It was in my "for the trash" shelf."

"The Spirit Lake Massacre and Captivity of Miss Abbie Gardner-Sharp. Look!

115

Written in 1885!" Roy was in heaven. "Thank you, dear wife!" With that, he gave her a very quick kiss and practically ran to his office at the other end of the house.

Sally sighed deeply. She smiled out loud because she finally had a relative that was in on a piece of family history. Until Roy brought it up, she had completely put the story of the massacre out of her mind. It was funny how that ancient-like story came back to her. It was Janet who had been her buddy in Iowa, and it was Janet's great-grandmother who broke the news that Sally and Janet were related. They were barely cousins, fourth or fifth cousins, but nevertheless related. The massacre was in 1857 when Janet and Sally's great, great, great, great grandmother, give or take a "great" or two, that was the common mother.

* * * * *

Next morning, Roy went into his office. There were several books and the usual raft of papers on his desk that he had only glanced at. And it was this he planned to tackle that day. He shuffled the mess, picked up the first pile and began to read. After about half an hour of this none of this seemed to have any meaning to him. He quit reading the confusion, but he was about to throw them down in disgust when he caught site of Sally's book peeking out from another pile of papers. Instead of throwing down the bunch in his hand, he laid them down gently, picked up the book, and began to read.

* * * * *

Spring, 1857

Even though it was still dark out, spring was a suggestion that Abbie Gardner couldn't ignore. She got up before the cows needed to be milked and decided to take a walk outside. The grass was still covered by a layer of snow, but, unlike her expectations, it was still cold, and she hurried back into the cozy log cabin for her shawl.

"I thought you knew better than to go outside alone this time of day," came a voice. Abbie looked around quickly and saw her mother at the fireplace about to start baking for breakfast.

"Yes, ma'am," Abbie said. "Sorry, but I didn't think there was any harm..."

"Our neighbors are Indians after all. I don't worry about the Winnebagos, but the Sioux can be wicked." Her mother stopped what she was doing long enough to observe, "What in the world made you get up this early? It's usually a tussle getting you out of bed at all."

"Oh, it's the beginning of spring, and I guess I had the fever. I needed to breathe outside air for a little while."

"You must always keep in mind that a band of renegades led by Inkpaduta is out there, and he is still looking for revenge for the murder of his brother, Sidominadotah."

"We haven't seen an Indian all winter," Abbie complained.

"The Sioux are trained in stealth and warfare and know how and when to become invisible. Besides, it's been a rough winter for them and will steal whatever food they can find, and they'll kill for it if need be. Now, will you please go and wake your brother and sister?"

"Papa, too?"

"Yes, Papa, too."

Before she could literally drag her little brother out of bed, Abbie could smell the biscuits in the oven. When she was a little girl, that was her signal to get up. If she got out of bed early enough, she could have the first biscuit right out of the oven, but best of all, she could have her mother all to herself even if it was just a few minutes.

Their cabin was small, but no smaller than any of their neighbors. And everyone would gather in front of the fireplace to shed the cold from their bones. So, it was a treat to have the comfort of Mama alone.

"Hurry, Abbie! The biscuits are done and hot, and I made a pot full of oatmeal. We must eat it before it gets too sticky."

Although Abbie was only 14, she could manage to get her siblings out of their beds and dressed quicker than her older sister Eliza and younger brother Rowland was able. She had another sister, Mary, who had married a few years ago and, in due time, had a little boy and a girl. She had missed her older sister as they had moved to Ohio, but they also heard the call of the West and came to Western Iowa to homestead. Unable to secure a place to stay, they bunked with Mama and Papa. Yes, Abbie mused, it was crowded, especially when her little niece and nephew were underfoot. But it was much better to have them indoors than to have them camping out in the cold and in danger of Inkpaduta and his band of warriors.

The news didn't travel very fast in that community as Abbie's nearest neighbor was a mile away, and the Sioux knew it. In fact, they were counting on it. Unknown to Abbie's family, Inkpaduta's raiders were already at work. At least they had not murdered anyone yet, but they shot the settler's livestock, and the squaws carried off the wheat and corn that the family used to exist. When they went up the Little Sioux River, they committed the same type of behavior at random, first by showing friendship and asking for food. As this method proved successful with other whites, the Sioux used it over and over. When the warrior was done eating, he lost the friendly demeanor and started demanding whatever caught his eye. The whites didn't take to this thievery and began to fight back. Gunshots were heard from outside where the Sioux were killing the livestock and carrying away anything they could. Then they would start on the settlers.

Despite this being old news to Abbie's family, they were sure that the Sioux had settled down after all that time. But time didn't prove to be on their side. On March sixth, Abbie's brother-in-law, Harvey, came back after his trip to Waterloo, and the next day Papa was going to prepare to go to Ft. Dodge for provisions.

The sun had never seemed brighter and the day friendlier on that March eighth. Papa was up early to get as many miles behind him as possible before sunset. They were about to sit down for breakfast, when a Sioux warrior boldly came in the door, demanding food. Quickly a place was set for him, and he was given breakfast including Mama's biscuits. He seemed friendly and kept his demands modest. That is, until he was done eating. Without warning, more Indians followed until Inkpaduta, and his fourteen warriors entered along with their squaws and papooses. The guise of friendship was suddenly dropped, and the warriors became insolent and demanding ammunition, food and anything that caught their fancy.

When Papa was doling out a few gun-caps, an Indian grabbed the entire box. Another tried to get the powder horn, but Harvey Luce prevented it. The Indian drew up his gun and would have shot Harvey had he not grabbed his gun pointed at the Indian's head.

Knowing that Papa was going to Ft. Dodge for provisions, neighbors Dr. Harriot and Mr. Snyder brought some letters that they wanted mailed. Papa told them what was going on and that other settlers should be warned of the danger. But Dr. Harriot and Mr. Snyder said they thought the Indians would tire of this game and go away and they left and went home, taking no precautions for themselves. By noon, the Indians went off toward Mr. Mattock's house. They also took the cattle and shot them on the way. Two hours later, they heard a gunshot in the direction of Mr. Mattock's house.

Papa was nervous with a lot of pent-up energy and went outside to have a look around. He soon rushed in saying that nine Indians were coming, and all the family was doomed as we had only two loaded guns. Almost immediately, the Indians stormed in and demanded the rest of the flour. As Papa went to fulfill that command, he was shot in the heart and fell dead. As her sister Mary seized one of the guns, the other Indians caught Mama and Mary by the arms and beat them over the head with their gun butts, dragged them outside, and finished killing them in a most shocking way.

The house soon became their source of amusement. They destroyed everything in the house by breaking open trunks and slicing into feather beds until feathers were all over everything in the house.

As she witnessed the destruction, she was seated in a chair holding her sister's baby girl in her arms with her brother on one side of her and her little nephew on the other. All were shaking with terror. The Indians came and jerked them away from her, took them outside as they were pleading with her for help, and beat them to death.

Being left alone, she found she had no desire to keep living, and I begged them to kill her. But it was now, as they grabbed her by the arms, she realized she had been taken into captivity.

Chapter 12

"Did I tell you what happened this morning when I went to the gym? It was so funny!" Sally's grin told Roy this one was going to be a lulu.

"True or False?"

"Oh, it's true. You can ask anyone who was there. "I'm sure it's a riot," Roy said with a slight smile and a disbelieving attitude.

"Well, I pulled a good one on Gene."

"Whose Gene?"

"He's the receptionist," Sally said with exasperation.

"Okay, okay, I'm sorry. Get along with the story."

"When I got there, there was no snow anywhere. Of course, you know that it's still early for snow, but it happens. And it happens that Gene is from Arizona and has never seen snow falling. So, when it started to snow just as I got to the gym, I pointed out to him that I brought the snow just for him, but it would stop when I left.

Roy began to laugh, a hearty, boisterous laugh. "You told him that?!" He asked as soon as he could catch his breath. Then he began to laugh again. Finally, he got ahold of himself and said between breaths, "How in this world did you manage that?" It stopped snowing as soon as she left the gym.

"Hey," Roy said in his "gotta go" voice, "I really need to get moving. I have a whole chapter that is squeezing out of my ears, and if I don't get it to paper soon, it's going to die."

"And we sure don't want that to happen. Go pump some life into that story, and I'll make you something fabulous for lunch."

Roy obediently kissed her, turned, and walked into his office like Dr. Frankenstein's assistant.

* * * * * *

In the late afternoon they took Abbie to Mr. Mattock's house where the darkness was pierced by campfires and the burning cabin. Dr. Harriot, Mr. Snyder, Mr. Mattock, and the bodies of others, totaling five men, two women, and four children lay outside. In the burning cabin, two other poor souls were suffering a fiery death. On the southern shore of East Okoboji, Mr. Clark and Abbie's brother-in-law, Harvey, were found shot. All in all, twenty human lives had been obliterated that day.

It was night by the time the Indians and Abbie reached their camp. All night the Indians danced in a hideous manner with war-whoops that made her blood freeze in her veins.

She was left alone in the tepee save for a nasty looking squaw who liked to hit her across the mouth if she made any noise. Abbie had been directed to braid her hair and dress like a squaw so she would fit into the tribe more and be invisible to the whites. They took away her shoes and gave her moccasins. That way her footprints could tell no tale.

Suddenly, a warrior in full make up came into the tepee. He wore a malevolent smile, and he sat down next to Abbie making her gag at his foul-smelling presence. He drew out a handgun and started to load it letting her know that as soon as he was done, he was going to shoot her. When he finished, he raised the gun, cocked it, and Abbie simply bowed her head to let him know that she was ready. The Indian slowly lowered the gun and left the tepee. It came back to her that the warrior that was going to shoot her took her head bowing as a sign of courage, and he couldn't kill her – he admired her too much.

The next morning, after spending a sleepless night on the ground inside the tepee, she was shaken by the squaw who guarded her the night before. The squaw motioned for her to get up and get to work. Abbie was given what appeared to be a bowl of watery-looking oatmeal, and not much of that. She refused to eat and was disciplined by the squaw with a hard, back-handed smack across the mouth.

Abbie was very tired after her night of no sleep, but she was put to work gathering artichokes by the river. She thought of just walking away, and if she died in the snow, then she would die. It would be better than being a captive. But if she did that, it would be the Indians that had won, and she couldn't suffer that. She would live to see this through and would go free!

Days upon days, move upon move, she endured the beatings and the tramping with the Indians carrying a seventy-pound backpack. She was eventually joined by three other captives, all she knew as neighbors, Mrs. Noble, Mrs. Thatcher, and Mrs. Marble. Abbie wasn't allowed to see them much except when they were out working, but those times were precious: being with friends and speaking English was such a treat.

Abbie learned that a male Indian does no work. He hunts, but only when the tribe is desperate for food, and that's the extent of it. Mostly he smokes, naps, and eats while the women do all the work. He would never lower himself to do work. That's a woman's job, and she is treated like a slave. As for the captives, they treated like a slave to the slaves.

As captives, they were not given the luxury of snowshoes, and they sank up to their waists in snow, or worse, water in creeks and gullies. The captives all had their packs to carry, but Mrs. Marble was also given a two-year-old papoose to carry in addition to what was strapped in her pack. When it fell asleep, Mrs. Marble would watch for an opportunity and reach back and claw the child. Of course, he would wake up and cry, and he did so often that one of the squaws figured the child didn't like white women, so she reached in and took that filthy baby away, just as Mrs. Marble had hoped. Mrs. Thatcher became ill with fever and all kinds of manifestations. She had been nursing her child, but now there was no babe to take the pressure off, and one of her swollen breasts broke. One limb became black, and the pressure that it caused made her veins burst. The Indians thought they would let her ride a horse instead of walk, but that turned out to be painful too. Finally, the medicine man worked on her and gave her some relief.

The Indians camped near the border of Iowa and Minnesota and left us alone with the squaws for several days. The warriors went to Springfield to continue their murderous ways and bring back as much booty as they could carry. The captives knew what was going to happen, and Mrs. Marble said she wished there was a way she could warn the settlers. It was a pipe dream. When the Indians came back, they were loaded with goods they had stolen, but to the captives, they were glad they didn't bring any more hostages.

Right away the squaws doused the fires with water, pulled down the tepees, gathered the plunder, and moved the women and children into the forest. The men positioned themselves to be able to see what would happen. A few hours later, a company of United States soldiers showed up. The captives were held in a place where they couldn't see the army, and they were told that if a battle ensued, all of them would be shot. The soldiers spent time looking at the abandoned campsite, and then, apparently, decided they would go back to Springfield. Their half breed guides told them the trail was several days old and trying to find them would be useless. The hostages were lucky that day.

Since the Indians reasoned that there would be no attack, their only interest was escaping from the soldiers. There was no time for rest or food. They didn't camp for two days and nights. Finally, Abbie's strength completely failed her, and she lay down on the ground. The Indians demanded that she get up and follow them, but she didn't pay any attention to their threats. All her fear of death, after all the suffering she had been through, had left her, so when one of the squaws threatened her with an Indian hoe, she simply bowed her head and waited for the anticipated blow. When the squaw saw that it didn't faze her, she threw down her pack, jerked her to her feet by her arm, and gave her a tremendous push in the back that sent Abbie in the direction of the others.

And that ended the escape from the soldiers, but their attempt only made things worse for the captives. There was no protection from wading through ice-cold water that was waist deep. Without changing into something dry, they were expected to live and sleep in the icy garments.

It took about six weeks marching over the prairie to reach the Big Sioux in Minnesota. In the meantime, spring had finally come in the guise of the snow melting which made walking easier, but it also meant that the rapid thawing of the snow filled the rivers and streams to overflowing.

On such a river, they attempted to cross over on a fallen tree, and they knew that one misstep could easily plunge them into icy waters. Mrs. Thatcher, after partially recovering from her black limb and the various illnesses and fevers, was made to carry a backpack. While crossing the stream, a young Indian, the same one who grabbed Abbie's father's box of shot, took Mrs. Thatcher's backpack from her, and added it to his own. This set off a red flag for both women. There was no kindness in this act, Mrs. Thatcher said, and said goodbye to Abbie. She was sure her time had come. When they reached the middle of the roaring water, the young Indian pushed her into the freezing water. Making a last grab at life, she somehow came up out of the torrent and grabbed a tree root. Here other Indians came at her throwing clubs and using long poles to push her back under the water. Then, when it appeared that she was going to make it across, she was beaten off again. She let the current carry her downstream all the while being pelted with sticks and rocks thrown by her tormentors. Following the bank as the current carried her, they ran into another bridge where one of the Indians finally shot her, ending her struggles. Her murder only served to remind Abbie of what cruel, misbegotten individuals these Sioux were.

Chapter 13

By her own reckoning, Abbie figured that it was about four weeks since Mrs. Marble had been sold and left, that they fell in line with another band of Sioux, a small party of Yanktons. One of them, by the name of Wanduskaihanke, which meant End-of-the-snake, purchased Mrs. Noble and Abbie. As with Mrs. Marble, her purchasers left the group, thus ending their time with Mrs. Marble. This Yankton continued to travel with Inkpaduta, but there were a few changes. For the first time, Mrs. Noble and Abbie were allowed to lodge in the same tepee, but their new owner treated them about the same as their former masters.

A few days after they were sold, the two women were about to lie down and rest when one of Inkpaduta's sons, Makpeahotoman, which meant Roaring Cloud, came into the Yankton's tepee and ordered Mrs. Noble to come out. Much to Abbie's horror, Mrs. Noble flatly refused. Abbie urged her to go saying if she didn't, they were both likely to end up dead. But Mrs. Noble stuck to her guns and refused again.

Roaring Cloud grabbed Mrs. Noble by the arm dragging her from the tepee. He brandished a very large wooden stick, and Abbie had no doubt what was going to happen. Abbie could only listen in silence to the blows and Mrs. Noble's groans that she endured. After that, the Indian, with his bloody hands, came into the tent, spoke to the Yankton, then lay down to sleep. Abbie had to listen to Mrs. Nobel's groans until all went silent. She wished she could go to her side, but she was too terror stricken by what had just happened, and even if she could, she was sure she would suffer the same end.

When morning came, the Sioux gathered around what was left of Mrs. Noble, amusing themselves with her as the target

127

of their bullets, then cutting off her hair and mutilating her body.

Now, being alone, Abbie began to lose track of time, something she had resolved not to do. She reckoned it was the bloody horror she witnessed coupled with the complete exhaustion with the never-ending toil, and having no one to talk to, she later wondered why she didn't break down completely.

Despite being as far down in the depths of despair as one could get, she somehow managed. She carried her heavy pack through sad and weary days heading in a general northwesterly direction. They crossed what appeared to be an endless prairie. No matter what direction she looked, all she could see was a grassy plain that ended on the horizon. But a positive was also there, a supply of buffalo, birds and wild fowl, and every day turned into a feast day, even for Abbie.

It was only a few days after Mrs. Noble's death when the group reached the St. James River. There was found a huge encampment of Yankton Sioux, maybe two thousand of them. Abbie was probably the first white person these people had ever seen, and she was a great curiosity to them. Some peeped through the door of the tepee, but other bold ones walked right in, inspecting her carefully. This went on as long as she was there.

It was the very end of May, and the Yankton's were still crowding into the tepee to look at Abbie, better known as "the white squaw," when three Indians dressed in coats and white shirts appeared in the tent. Much as she wanted to talk to them, she dared not, and they made no attempt to talk to her. She had no idea what it was all about, but it came later she learned it was about her. The men in suits and the Yanktons gathered around her tent and talked, then they took their council out in the prairie where they sat in a circle and smoked and talked which seemed to be endless. It went on for three days.

Abbie was told by Inkpaduta's men and the Yanktons of the horrible fate that was awaiting her. They seemed to be amused to talk about burning her alive, dragging her to the river where they would drown her, or chopping her up alive into little pieces starting with her toes. Knowing that these were probably lies, Abbie didn't listen. It wasn't until a squaw somehow imparted to her that these "tortures" were lies that Abbie lost a little of her fear.

The Indian council finally came to a conclusion. They would seek the whites for arbitration since they didn't completely trust the "coats and suites." They decided to put her price at two horses, twenty pounds of tobacco, thirty-seven and a half yards of calico and ribbon, twelve blankets, thirty-two yards of blue squaw cloth, two kegs of powder and other sundries.

Once the price had been paid, Abbie was immediately turned over to the new purchasers. To seal and celebrate the transaction, there was nothing of a higher honor than dog-feast. Abbie had no interest in this feast and stayed in her tepee. She knew she was taking a chance to be rude not to take part in the feast. She was still uncertain as to what would happen next, but it was her last night with the Yanktons. She was thankful to rid herself of Inkpaduta and his band who had murdered those so dear to her.

Inkpaduta, Abbie noted a few years later, that he was one of the Indians that participated in the battle that was dubbed, "Custer's Last Stand."

After six days journey, Abbie, and her new owners, the Yanktons, reached St. Paul on June 22. Here she would be turned over to the governor, or, as the Indians would say, "The Great Father." There they were met by a large crowd who cheered her appearance. The next morning, June 23, she was formally turned over to the governor. There were speeches, more cheers, and the governor, of course, made a long speech.

Then she was free.

* * * * *

"Well?" Sally said in a baffled voice.

"Well, what?" Roy answered.

"What happened after that? I mean, what happened to her? Where did she go? What did she do? You just can't end it like that!"

"Lots of things end like that."

Sally heaved a big sigh. She knew now he was stringing her along.

"What was the first thing she did?"

"Oh, is that what you want to know! Why didn't you just say so?"

Sally punched him playfully in the arm. "Yes, that and many other things. If you just leave her hanging like that, you're going to get some angry mail."

"Probably not angry mail, just frustration in an envelope."

"So, tell me! Where did she go and do first?"

Roy relented on holding back just to amuse himself, so he continued. "Abbie was invited to join the governor's family, to adopt her and make her his daughter. But, as good as the offer was, she had another that was even better. Abbie had found her sister.

"Her sister? I thought her whole family was murdered by Inkpaduta's renegade bunch."

"I guess you don't remember that her older sister, Eliza, wasn't home that week, so she escaped the massacre."

"Thank goodness! So, she went home. That's so nice."

"No, she couldn't go home," Roy said simply. "All she knew about Eliza was she was alive and had gotten married. She had to do some searching. Abbie knew her sister was living in Iowa, but that's a lot of territory to cover. But, with all the influential people she knew now, they helped Abbie find her. Eliza was in Hampton, a town in north central Iowa, not near anything. I'll bet the population isn't much bigger than it is now."

"So, she found her sister," Sally said thoughtfully. But what did she do for the rest of her life?"

"What most women did at that time. She married Casville Sharp and had three children that kept her from getting bored. As time slipped away, her kids grew up, and she lived with her husband until her death in 1921. Ultimately, in 1891, she bought the house her family lived in until Inkpaduta changed everything. She created a museum and gave tours, sold trinkets she made herself, and a good number of her books she titled The Spirit Lake Massacre and Captivity of Miss Abbie Gardner. Her family still lies where they were so hastily buried so long ago."

"Do you think we could go there sometime?"

"Sure. But what about your asthma?"

"I'll have a good long talk with Dr. Tremble. I'm sure that she could do something for me."

"All in all, what do you think of this?" Roy asked with an honest inquiry in his eyes.

"It needs all that information added to the ending. An epilogue, I guess you would call it."

"And an epilogue it will have. Thanks for your input." He kissed her, gathered up his papers, and headed for his office.

Chapter 14

April 8, 1865

President and Mrs. Lincoln had been vacationing in City Point, VA for two weeks, but he was needed now in Washington. Even so he wanted to wait for General Lee to surrender. City Point was General Grant's supply center and a meeting place between Grant and Lincoln. The President liked it as it was away from Washington and its pressures, but Mary Lincoln was uncomfortable there.

Since Lincoln's arrival in City Point, the telegrams he received from Grant and Sherman kept the President informed. During this time, Richmond had been captured, and Petersburg had been evacuated. But most important was Lee's Army was in the final stages of surrender.'

But before he left, he wanted to visit their hospital. Lincoln visited all he could of the wounded in several hundred tents and about a hundred wooden barracks. He shook hands with all he could, most of the men asked how the war was going, and his reply was, "Success all along the line."

While Lincoln was scheduled to depart City Point for Washington, he had to attend a reception aboard the River Queen. With all the handshaking expected at the reception plus the handshaking he had endured at the hospital, he confessed to his wife that "...my arms ache tonight."

After the reception, the River Queen's lights were dimmed, and the party decoration removed, and it began steaming down the James River toward Chesapeake Bay. It was accompanied by the USS Bat, the only heavily armed ship that might be able to keep up with the River Queen.

Admiral Porter's instructions assigned Commander Barnes, two officers, and a detachment of enlisted men to guard the President, day and night. Porter had heard many rumors of assassination plots, and, as long as Lincoln was on the River Queen, he and the Navy were held responsible for the President's welfare.

April 9, 1865

The River Queen steamed north to the Potomac. The USS Bat's boilers "foamed up" when there was a change from salt water to fresh, and she couldn't keep up with the Queen, that arrived several hours before the Bat.

Because there had been no news from shore about the war, it was a relaxing time for Lincoln. When they passed Mt. Vernon, someone remarked how lovely it would be for the President when he could return to Springfield. Lincoln agreed by saying, "It would be like awakening from a trance." Finishing his last four years was his dream so he could "...return there in peace and tranquility." He assured his company that there would be no more fighting during his second term.

6:00 PM

The River Queen docked in Washington, and a while later the USS Bat. They found the people were excited. Bonfires were everywhere. The Lincoln's had been aboard the River Queen all day, no one had heard any news. The driver of the Lincoln's carriage stopped the rig and asked a passerby what all the excitement was about. The man didn't recognize Lincoln, but he answered, "Where have you been? Lee has surrendered!"

April 10, 1865

Morning

Lincoln's bodyguard, William Crook, reported for work Monday morning only to find out the President was up and sitting at his desk going through his unanswered mail. Since the excitement of the past few days had passed, Lincoln's stress was making itself more obvious. Having gone for seventeen days meant there were seventeen days of work that had to be read and answered. And, as usual, whenever the President was in the White House, the same kind of visitors crowded in. Some just wanted to shake his hand and congratulate him on Lee's surrender. Then there were those who came to advise him on dealing with Confederates. In addition, there was the usual bunch looking for jobs and appointments.

Afternoon

While Lincoln was still going through the accrued paperwork, a crowd moved on to the lawn of the White House and began calling out for the President. Along with the crowd were members of the Quartermaster's band who played some wonderful music. With that, Lincoln came to the window and spoke to a large number of people. But so he didn't disappoint anyone, he called on the band to play "Dixie," one of Lincoln's favorites. And it came along with the surrender as a spoil of war. When Lincoln told this to a crowd, there was tremendous laughter and applause.

Having been at the window long enough, the President ducked back inside and went back to work. A few hours later, another crowd came to the window calling for Lincoln. This time he was able to turn them away with a few laughable remarks.

6:00 PM

A group of fifteen young men came to the White House and Lincoln met them just inside the door. Each was introduced, and the man who made the introductions made a short speech. It was a very patriotic speech that the President politely listened to. Then they presented Lincoln with a portrait of himself with an elaborate silver frame. He remarked, "You did your best. It wasn't your fault that the frame is so much more rare than the picture."

April 11, 1865

Much of the day was used by Lincoln getting ready for the speech he would give that evening.

9:00 AM

Lincoln issued a proclamation closing more than thirty ports in Alabama, Florida, Louisiana, Mississippi, Texas, and Virginia. They would remain closed until they were opened up by the President.

One of the things that the President was trying to say was that during the war, the United States had expanded and had, without doubt, become naval power being equal to any other.

Evening

The speech Lincoln was planning for the evening was his central activity for the day. All the public buildings in town were lit by candles and lamps. Even Robert E. Lee's former home was lit. In fact, the whole city was blazingly brilliant.

Along Pennsylvania Ave, the only paved street at the time, thousands of people made their way to the White House. The Avenue was clogged with people and the sidewalks between 15th and 17th streets were blocked.

Lincoln gave his speech from a window in the White House. The lighting was not good and holding his speech in one hand and a candle in the other proved to be terribly awkward. Finally, he gestured to news correspondent Noah Brooks to help him out. Brooks, holding the candle so Lincoln could use both hands for the speech, worked out well.

The very first part of the speech concerned a mention of Appomattox and Petersburg, and there would be a "natural Thanksgiving." But the start, as uplifting as it was, shifted to the topic of reconstruction, something "fraught with difficulty."

At the end of the speech, the crowd cheered and applauded, but there seemed to be a lack of enthusiasm. Apparently, the crowd was expecting a victory speech, and not a long, winding speech about Louisiana legislation and reconstruction.

The speech was printed in the newspaper, sometimes edited, sometimes the full text. But most of the papers remarked about the cheering crowd and the candles, lamps, and other sources of light, but other papers, like the New York Tribune said the speech "...caused great disappointment and left a painful impression."

April 12, 1865

Sunrise

The surrender ceremony called for lines formed by sunrise, and General Chamberlain watched as the Confederate forces took down their tents for the last time. The surrender ceremony lasted all day: Confederate units came forward, surrendered their flags and weapons, then withdrew.

Morning - Afternoon

Even though Washington was still celebrating the surrender, it was a normal workday for Lincoln and his staff. One item was a pardon for a member of the Forty-Sixth New York Volunteers for desertion. Lincoln asked that the man be returned to his regiment with no death sentence. The President also asked Secretary of War Stanton to give to one of his own a recommendation to West Point. He also sent a telegram to General Godfrey Weitzel concerning a reprimand to the General because he had not ordered prayers for the President to be said all over Richmond.

Evening

With all the warnings of assassination attempts, Lincoln's sleep was deeply affected. In a recent dream, it was so frightening that he kept it to himself for a few days. When he was finally able to talk about it, Mary Lincoln wanted to hear about it as much as the President wanted to talk about it.

In his dream, it started with a disturbed sleep, and he dreamed he heard "disturbed sobs." The sobbing afflicted him so much that he dreamed he got out of bed and went downstairs and there he heard more "subdued sobs," but he couldn't see anyone. Going from room to room, he found no one in sight util he finally found himself in the East Room. There he saw a catafalque that held a corpse "wrapped in funeral vestments." Finally, he asked the soldiers who it was. The soldier answered, "The President. He was killed by an assassin." This remark was followed by "a large burst of grief" from the people in the room, and it woke Lincoln up. He was not able to sleep anymore that night and left him strangely annoyed by the dream ever since.

April 13, 1865

Morning

Although President Lincoln was not in the most festive of moods, he thought, in a way to cheer himself up, he would go for a horseback ride around Washington.

The President, on his way through town, happened to come across assistant Secretary of the Treasury, Maunsell B. Field, who was taking a carriage ride. Secretary Field noticed that Lincoln was in a mood of enormous melancholy with the look penetrating weariness from him.

Despite his mood, Lincoln rode off back to the White House and took care of some simple paperwork. His day also included an important meeting with Secretary of War Stanton, and the second most popular person in the country, General U.S. Grant, Lincoln being first.

The meeting's subject was the final disposition of the war. It was agreed, now, that General Lee had surrendered, that there would be no more battles or campaigns. That was just what President Lincoln wanted to hear.

Unlike her husband, Mary Lincoln told the New York Herald's James Gordon Bennett that, "We are rejoicing beyond expression over our great and glorious victories." Mary's mood was cheerful, and now that her son Robert was home, there would be no more strain and anxiety to her husband's health. The President was in quite poor shape. He was probably about thirty pounds underweight, appearing gaunt and frail to everyone. Mary hoped, now that the war was nearly over, that her husband would be restored in health.

After breakfast with Mary and Robert, Lincoln went to his office. Senator John P. Hale of New Hampshire was his first meeting, then a visit from a Detroit attorney William Alanson

Howard. After that, there was a meeting with California Congressman Cornelius Cole. Following, Mr. Cole was Speaker of the House Schyler Colfax who was interested in becoming a member of Lincoln's cabinet. The President then sent messages to Secretary of State William Seward and General Grant, both notes contained memorandum about that morning's cabinet meeting at 11:00.

With the cabinet meeting starting on time, Frederick Stewart, the assistant Secretary of State who took his father's place at the meeting since his father was still too incapacitated from being attacked by an assassin's blade.

The talk at the meeting was, of course, the war, and if there was any news from General William Tecumseh Sherman in North Carolina. General Grant informed the group that he had not received any recent news from General Sherman. By not hearing any news from General Sherman, it meant that General Joseph E. Johnson and his army were still at large. But Lincoln assured them all that he could, at any moment, receive a message from North Carolina containing Joe Johnson's surrender.

Another item on the agenda was having North Carolina and Virginia restored to the Union. Secretary Wells objected because Virginia already had a legitimate state government thanks to Governor Francis Pierpont. This and many other ideas were discussed. All these ideas had to be discussed when there was full membership at the next meeting.

Afternoon

At the end of the meeting, about 2:00, when everyone was shaking hands with each other, Lincoln asked General Grant if he and his wife, Julia, would like to accompany him and Mrs. Lincoln to see "Our American Cousin" at Ford's theater that evening. Grant declined the invitation saying they were going to New Jersey to visit their children. Many others were invited but turned down the offer. Finally, Major Henry R. Rathbone and fiancée Clara Harris accepted.

General Joe Johnson finally gave in and surrendered. The news of Johnson's capitulation did not reach Washington that day.

That afternoon, a flag raising was held at Fort Sumter in Charleston Harbor. It was Good Friday and the very same flag that had been surrendered to General P.G.T. Beauregard four years ago was raised again. The ceremony was meant to mark the end of the war.

The Republican National Convention called on President Lincoln to ask him how the best way was to select a running mate, but Lincoln was told they had already chosen Andrew Johnson. The President said, "Cannot interfere about platform." Lincoln thought very little of Johnson. In fact, he was entirely noncommittal and wouldn't endorse him or reject him. The Lincoln – Johnson conference began after the cabinet meeting, and later the President had lunch with Johnson and his wife.

Lincoln also had an unscheduled meeting with a black lady named Nancy Bushrod who had been a slave "...on the old Harwood Plantation near Richmond." Tom, her husband, and their three small children were dependent on Tom's soldier pay. But the pay had stopped when Tom died, and Nancy was destitute and needed her husband's pay to be restored. At the White House, two sets of guards attempted to keep Nancy out, but the woman and the guards began shouting at each other, and it gained President Lincoln's attention who told the guards, "There is time for all who need me. Let the good woman come in." Her husband's pay was reinstated.

On a short walk to the War Department with his personal bodyguard, William Crook, Lincoln said, "I believe there are men who want to take my life, and I have no doubt they will do it." The statement upset and frightened Crook, and the only thing he could think of to say was, "I hope you are mistaken, Mr. President."

Dinner at the White House was served earlier that night to give the Lincolns time enough to get to the theater. After dinner, Mary complained about a headache and said she really didn't want to go out. He said that another night would result in callers all evening and would not be enjoyable or quiet. Mary agreed to go to the theater.

Evening

As the presidential party entered the theater at 8:30, they were late as the play had already started. The orchestra immediately stopped playing for the comedy on stage and went into "Hail to the Chief." Once in the box, Lincoln acknowledged the applause and cheers from the audience.

The Lincolns enjoyed the play with the President laughing out loud and Mary applauded the action on stage.

When the comedy was nearly over in the third act, a loud noise came from the presidential box. Later the audience would say it sounded more like a "crack" and not a "bang." There was no one who thought it was a gunshot. The strange noise, which happened at 10:13, proceeded a man with a knife in his hand that jumped out of the presidential box. The jump was awkward with the spur on his right foot catching on the bunting that hung across the outside of the box. He landed on his left foot quite heavily. After falling forward on his hands, he shouted, "Sic semper tyrannis!", but others said it was "The South is avenged!"

When Major Rathbone tried to stop the intruder, Booth dropped his derringer and pulled out a dagger, slashing Rathbone's arm to the bone. Shouting something about revenge for the South, Booth jumped out of the Presidential box and on to the stage. It was then that Mary Lincoln realized what had happened and shouted, "They have shot the President!" over and over.

Despite the chaos, a young army surgeon, Charles A. Leale, managed to reach the box and found Lincoln slumped over in his rocker. Dr. Leale found the .44 caliber bullet hole where the shot had entered the skull.

A clot that was forming around the bullet hole was cleared by the doctor. Another army doctor, Dr. Charles Taft, was admitted to the box. Both doctors agreed that the wounds were mortal.

The box was too small and crowded for anyone much less a tall man with a bullet in his brain. Dr. Leale ordered six soldiers to carry Lincoln out of the theater and to the home of William Petersen across the street. He was taken to a small bedroom and laid diagonally across the bed because he was too tall to fit lengthwise.

When Mary Lincoln saw her husband, she screamed saying she wanted Tad, and then she shouted that she herself should have been the one shot. Mrs. Lincoln was taken to another room where she could cry her heart out.

General Grant, on his way to New Jersey to visit his children, was contacted that he was needed back in Washington. Not only was the President fighting for his life, but also Secretary of State Seward and his son were gravely wounded.

April 15, 1865

Wee hours of the morning

Robert Lincoln had joined the overcrowded room at the Petersen's house, he stood at the head of the bed. Robert could see that the President was nearing the end. By 1:00 AM, the doctors pronounced him brain dead. He was finally pronounced dead at 7:22 AM. Secretary Stanton, in his own way, said, "Now he belongs to the ages."

Chapter 15

It was about 4:00 AM two weeks later when Roy and Sally were awakened by sirens and flashing lights.

"Sally, get up! I think the Lockerbee's house is on fire!"

"But that's practically next door!"

"We have a whole empty lot between us and them."

"I'd say that we have a whole empty full of dried garden leftovers," she reminded him.

"Whatever. I'm going to get dressed and see what I can do to help."

"Good idea. I'm going to make a space in the family room, so they have a place to live temporarily."

"That's great," Roy said as he jammed his arms in the sleeves of his jacket. He ran out the door, and Sally watched as he became a dark shadow against the height of the flames.

Sally had always been terrified of fire. She somehow tolerated the fire in the fireplace, but to give the blaze any kind of leeway, she needed to put it out or run away from it. She couldn't put this one out, and she couldn't run away from it. She looked out the family room window, and to her relief, the fire seemed to be under control with only a few flames coming out of the Lockerbee's upstairs bathroom window.

An hour later, Roy came back home carrying a laundry bag full of something. Sally's questioning look encouraged Roy to explain without even asking.

"It's a bag of 'treasures' that Heather couldn't bear to leave behind. There will be more. It seems that their boy Milo was awake when the fire started, and he yelled for the family to get up. That early warning gave them a few more seconds to round up what they wanted."

"Do they know the cause of the fire yet?"

"Donald said, according to the firefighters, it was electrical. They need a temporary place to stay, and I invited them here. Have you found any space?"

"I turned the family room into a shelter. It should work since the downstairs bathroom is right there and the kitchen just beyond. By the way, how long is 'temporary?'"

"A day or two. Heather's mother lives on the other side of town."

"While you were over at Donald and Heather's," Sally mused, "especially with all that dried up garden between us, why didn't the fire spread? You know, like the Chicago Fire did back in 1871. Didn't they have fire equipment and firefighters then?"

"Oh," Roy answered, "They had the most up-to-date fire equipment for the era. It was a matter of the elements and bad luck that made it spread. Those things were missing here, thank goodness."

A knock at the back door alerted them that the Lockerbees had arrived. Sally let them in, looking bedraggled, confused, and wiped out. Their younger child, Marie, was crying.

"We couldn't save Marie's cat," Heather whispered to Sally.

With a sad smile, Sally said, "Well, we have two cats she can cuddle with. It might help."

The O'Malleys had known the Lockerbees for as long as they had lived so close, and Sally, on occasion, babysat for them. But who was this extra man that came in with the family?

"Oh, Sally," Heather said, "you haven't met Greg, a shirttail relative of Donald's. He came into town rather unexpectedly and has been staying with us." Heather touched Sally's arm and encouraged her to go into the kitchen.

"I really don't know how he's related," Heather confessed in a low voice. "All I know is that he claimed to be a third cousin once removed. Now, I can understand a third or fourth cousin, but when they start removing cousins, I'm lost. He doesn't say much, but when he does, it's all about genealogical ties. Says putting together families is a hobby, and that's how he found us. I'm not sure about his story, and I'm uncomfortable around him."

"Has he said how long he's going to stay with you?" Sally asked.

"Here's the creepy part: he says he must stay until he receives 'the signal.' I haven't got a clue what that means, but I really wish he would get that 'signal' sooner than later."

Sally helped the family get somewhat settled, and, despite the dawn, they all fell asleep right away.

She signaled to Roy to be very quiet and to follow her. They ended up in the living room on the other side of the house.

"I'm curious. What kind of firefighting equipment did they have back then? It couldn't have been anything like we have today."

"Believe it or not, they had the state-of-the-art. 1871 style, anyway." Roy stopped for a minute, then continued. "I thought you were going to tell me some deep, dark secret, and it appears that there is something like that."

"What was the population of Chicago then?" Sally asked ignoring his request for secret information.

"The year was 1865, just after the Civil War, with people trying to get their lives in order and find permanent places to live. Chicago just naturally got a big chunk of that. So, they had to come up with something that would be useful, practical, and uncomplicated for anyone who needed firefighters. The results were alarm boxes, 172 of them, installed throughout the city. To prevent false alarms, the city entrusted keys to the boxes to local citizens, usually a nearby shopkeeper, with the key. That way, when there was a fire, someone would have to go to the nearest shop or residence for a key, then that person would pull the switch. To get the firefighters to the right place, each box had a number. Say, number 125, and the key person would ring once, then twice, then five times. If flames were detected by the watchman on duty in the cupola of the Courthouse, he would alert another fireman at the station who would telegraph the operator in the Courthouse."

Sally sat amazed at her husband's knowledge. "That sounds like a waste of time, with all that handing off. Suppose the keykeeper was out of town or couldn't be located. What did they do then?"

"I don't know," Roy said flatly.

"And did Mrs. O'Leary's cow really kick over a lantern to start the fire?"

"Again, I don't know. But no one really knows what happened in that barn that night. The fire started, no doubt, in the O'Leary barn, but some put the blame on a neighbor, Peg Leg' Sullivan. Others think it was a bunch of youths trying to find a place to smoke. Nothing has ever been proven."

"When did it start and when did it end? And why did it spread so fast?"

"That is a whole 'nother story."

"Speaking of another story, I heard a beauty from Heather."

"Will this take long? I'd really like to get back to my dream."

Sally lowered her eyes, nodded, and said, "Let's just keep it for tomorrow. It'll hold."

*   *   *   *   *

9:00 PM

It was October 8, 1871, when O'Leary neighbor William Lee was the first to notify the fire department about the barn. It was, in this case, a quarter of a mile to get to Box 296 located at the corner of Twelfth Street (now Roosevelt Road) and Canal Street. After the shopkeeper had completed the number, Lee rushed back to DeKoven Street where the barn was located. Lee was confident help was on the way, but the alarm telegraph operator never received it.

9:10 PM

Another man went to the box where Lee had put in an alarm, and he was screaming, "The fire is spreading very rapidly!" So, the storekeeper tried again, but once more it failed.

Catherine O'Leary's cows and a horse became the Fire's first fatalities.

After the war, with the glut of people trying to find a home in Chicago, the houses and barns and just about everything else were made of wood, and they easily caught fire. Tar roofs and wood shavings also facilitated the blaze.

And then there was the wind. Chicago had witnessed the driest summer it had ever seen: no rain for weeks and a heat that included a whipping wind that encouraged the Fire. Anything made of wood, which included most buildings, were tinder-dry, licked by the hungry Fire.

9:30 PM

Saturday night there had been a tremendous fire in Chicago, and many engine companies had damaged engines and injured men. But, with the spirit of Chicago in his veins, acting captain William Musham, a rarity being an actual native of Chicago, recruited a few spectators to assist his men.

What was described as a roar, the wind picked up, blowing the streams of water

from hoses away from their targets while encouraging the flames on their way. It also produced "fire devils". As the wind continued to roar, it picked up cinders and even flaming chunks of wood that were hurled over their heads as the helpless firefighters looked on.

10:00 PM

One of those flaming chunks of wood wedged itself in the 140-foot wooden steeple of St. Paul's Catholic Church. Fire Chief William Marshall put three engines on the church. Unfortunately, the heat was intolerable, and they couldn't get close enough to do any good.

On the same block as the church was a furniture finishing company, a retail furniture company, a shingle mill, and a box factory. All of these were in two large warehouses. Both warehouses were full of flammable materials, and next to it was a thousand cords of wood stacked twenty-five feet high, 600,000 feet of furniture lumber, and 750,000 shingles. One firefighter described it as "The most combustible place in the city of Chicago."

One owner of such a building was determined to save his property, so he and two others soaked the building with water so the Fire would pass it over. It didn't, and the fire gobbled up his property.

11:00 PM

Joseph Medill, one of the owners of the Chicago Tribune, was awakened by one of his family. He anxiously looked out the window, saw the direction of the wind, and concluded that his home was not in any danger. He got dressed and went down in the panicking crowd and edged his way out onto the Randolph Street Bridge.

The Chief Fire Marshall was standing near the skeleton of a store when he was informed the Fire now extended over 150 acres and was three-quarters of a mile long. At this point he was also informed that the Fire was now on the South Side.

11:30 PM

Mayor Roswell B. Mason arrived at the Courthouse with one of his adult sons. He had come from his home about two miles away on the west side of Michigan Avenue

south of Twelfth Street. Realizing that he had very little time to act, he sent telegrams to other cities in the Upper Midwest appealing for emergency help.

12:00AM

James J. Hildreth, a Civil War veteran, insisted to Mayor Mason that the best way to stop the Fire was to blow up enough buildings to the fuel for the Fire had been cut off. Mayor Mason ignored the request. Chief Williams admitted he didn't know how to use powder and Mason absolutely did not. But Hildreth was stubborn enough to keep asking to use the powder, and he finally got it. He hauled the powder from a powder magazine he knew. Hildreth recruited a police sergeant and a group of officers to help him move the kegs across the street to LaSalle and Washington. He spread the powder and set the explosive off. And he did it at another building nearby. Much to his chagrin, the powder did little more than break some windows.

12:30 AM

In the slum district of Conley's Patch, a large blazing fragment hit and burst into flames turning the area into a tinder patch. Horace White, currently editor in chief of the Chicago Tribune, described those fleeing the inferno as "...a crowd of blear-eyed, drunken, and diseased wretches, male and female, half naked, ghastly, with painted cheeks, cursing and uttering ribald jests as they drifted along."

From that, the Parmelee, Chicago Gas and Light, and Conley's Patch fires merged.

Citizens began moving carts, filled with their furniture and goods, away from their doomed houses. One of those was the Carlson family. Their oldest child, Albert, had just graduated from high school, and he was very proud of the beautiful watch his parents had given him. Now that the house was in danger, and the cart ready to begin the task of finding somewhere the fire wasn't, Albert remembered his watch. He yelled to his mother, saying he was going back in to find it, and he headed for the stairs before she could stop him. Upstairs, the open windows facilitated the fire, but Albert was determined to find his watch. And there it was, sitting on his dresser. He grabbed it, jammed it in his pocket and ran back to the way he came up. This time, however, the fire had moved so fast that it was already climbing up the stairs. There was no other place to go. He ran back to the window that overlooked the street and yelled, "Hold the horse, I'm coming down!" Despite the protests of his parents, he jumped, landing on the upholstery of the fainting couch. It wasn't the best place to land, but the bruises and a broken bone in his hand, it was better than the alternative. The family found no refuge as everyone in the neighborhood was looking for the same thing. They ended up in Lake Michigan, hoping the water would save them. However, with all the flying, burning chunks and sparks blown by the wind, they had to do what other people had done: abandon their carts and wade into the water up to their necks trying not to drown by the wind-whipped waves. The family survived but not their goods. They had nothing left. Nothing but Albert's watch.

1:30AM

Mayor Mason and his son left the Courthouse where he had gone to save some papers. He discovered he was no different than ten thousand other Chicagoans all trying to survive. The mayor found that the way to his home was now blocked by blazing buildings. He and his son decided on a different route to get around the fire, but that soon became impossible with more streets quickly being taken over by the conflagration. His house was not far from the Courthouse, but it took him four hours to get home. And he was lucky.

2:00AM

In the Courthouse Cupola, watchman Mathias Schaefer along with telegraph operator William Brown, saw the Fire, that had seemed to be so removed just a while ago, had become too real and they would have to go if they didn't want to burn to death. The stairway was on fire, so they apparently jumped down.

While all this was going on, the fire in the cupola was eating away at the supports of its five-and-a-half-ton bell. With a crash that made the earth tremble up to a mile away, the bell was now screaming hot metal that tumbled to the burned-out courthouse floor below. It went silent.

Dawn

Robert Todd Lincoln, 26, son of the former president, was living in Chicago beginning his career as a corporate lawyer.

His house was safely out of the danger zone on South Wabash Avenue, and his mother, Mary Todd Lincoln, lived with him along with his two-year-old daughter and his wife, all named Mary. He had recently returned from a trip to the Rocky Mountains after the death of Tad Lincoln, his third and final sibling. Brother Eddie had died in 1850 at the age of three, and Willie, 11, died of typhoid while the family was living in the White House.

Lincoln put himself in danger to try and rescue some of the files in his office. He gathered all the files he could tote and wrapped up the papers in a tablecloth that he turned into a sack.

* * * * * *

Roy put his empty coffee mug down and offered more to Donald and Heather Lockerbee. Both answered affirmatively, and Sally poured. Greg was still sleeping, and Sally was about ready to go crazy about the cousin, but she somehow put a stop on it.

"I don't know why, but I have always been fascinated by that fire, and here you are researching it!" Heather said sadly. "We didn't have to drag our possessions blocks and blocks, we just started throwing things outside. My great-grandmother's dishes are even safe."

"What woke you up when the fire was just starting?" Sally asked.

"Ironically, it was Marie's cat. She jumped up and down on the bed until Marie woke up and smelled the smoke. Marie and Milo came running into our room and yelled. I called the fire department while ushering everyone outside. We even had time to grab our jackets. We somehow just forgot about Maya until Marie missed her. By that time, it was too late to go back in, even the fire department wouldn't go.

"You know you're more than welcome to stay with us until you can make other arrangements," Roy reminded them.

"And we thank you very much," Donald wearily nodded. "I'll get in touch with my mother when it's light."

"What does dawn have to do with it? She won't be annoyed at this kind of a phone call."

"You are so right, Heather. Sally, can I use your phone?"

"It's all yours."

When Donald went into the living room to get the phone, Sally asked Roy, "So what happened then? We're up at the early, early morning."

"You want more of my research?"

"Please, Roy," Heather sighed. It kinda makes our tragedy not seem so bad."

"Okay, then, here we go."

"Roy, wait, wait, wait! I want to hear more about Albert's watch."

"Really?"

"Considering the watch was saved, and he is your cousin, probably about 4 times removed by now, I want to know what happened to it."

"Not a lot to tell. I have no idea what Albert did with it, but I suppose he wore it."

"You mean he didn't try to sell it? After all, they had been wiped out and needed money."

"Oh, no, he kept it. I saw the watch on many occasions. However, Grandma told us the watch had stopped many years before, when she was a girl, and it couldn't be fixed. With nothing to lose, she gave it to her kids to play with.

That poor watch really took a beating. Then my generation came along and really messed it up. The glass was gone, the hands were popped and bent, and it didn't wind properly. When Grandma moved into a retirement home after Gramps died, I never saw it again. When I asked Grandma what happened to it, she said she gave it to the neighborhood jeweler who would give it to one of his apprentices to practice on. If they ever got it going again, he would return it. Grandma didn't have much hope to ever see it again, and she didn't. She lived to be 90 and passed quietly. What wonderful summers we had in Iowa with her and Gramps when I was a kid."

"It's so nice of you people to let us stay with you. Do you think anyone was offered the same luxury as you showed us?" Donald inquired.

"There were too many people who were out on the streets looking for shelter, and the other side of town, where there was no fire, but out of reach," Roy informed him.

"Were there any, for a lack of a better term, 'celebrities' killed by the Fire?" Heather asked.

"Oh, there were celebrities, many of them," Roy assured them. "Some did succumb, but others somehow survived. That Fire was a great leveler that didn't care about anyone's status. But the survivors that come to mind at the moment were John R. Chapman, artist for "Harper's Weekly, Joseph Edgar Chamberlin, a writer for the "Chicago Post," and Arthur M. Kinzie, grandson of a fur trader and one of the founders of Chicago. Another was James Bradwell, a Cook County judge, who tried to save his possessions by burying them. But my favorite was E.I. Tinkham of the Second National Bank who paid $6,000 for conveying him and a box with $600,000 in it. He considered the circumstances and decided it was worth it," Roy chuckled.

"So how did it all end? It sounds like the fire was too intense and there was a total lack of resources to put it out," Heather asked.

"That's right. It continued to burn that day and through the second night," Roy said sadly.

"So how did it get put out?" Donald almost begged.

"I think you two best get some more sleep. And when you wake up, Sally will have a nice breakfast for you," Roy said trying to hide his amusement.

"Oh, come on, neighbor!" Donald said in frustration.

"It's not a secret." Roy said simply.

"Well, then, tell us!" Heather begged.

"It rained."

Just about then, Cousin Greg came into the family room and said good morning, and everyone replied in one voice.

"What are you all talking about?

"Just chatting about one of your favorite subjects, the Chicago Fire," Heather informed him.

"Oh, the stories I could tell you about that event!

"Tell, tell!" the children begged.

"Let poor Cousin Greg have at least a cup of coffee and a bowl of cornflakes before he has to start picking his brain for you." Heather said.

"If you don't mind," Greg broke in, "I'd love to have French toast instead."

Sally could feel all the pairs of eyes on her, and she declared, "Aw, what the heck! French toast for everyone!"

After the last of the sticky syrup was wiped up, hands were washed and the dishes done, Sally sat down in the family room to take a breath before she got up to get into street clothes. With another family to feed she had to get to the grocery store. If what was eaten for breakfast was a sample of what to expect, she'll have to load up. She had left her wallet in the bedroom, so she hurried upstairs to grab it. She also encountered Heather.

"Where are you going this early," Heather asked her.

"Truth be told, I'm going to the grocery store."

"I was afraid of that. Let me come along and I'll help with the bill. And don't let me hear you protest. Donald and I talked it over and we decided you shouldn't bear the burden of the food we eat. We can split the bill. And I mean it!"

Properly cowed, Sally agreed.

Sometime later, with double the bags hauled into the house, Heather sat down in one of the kitchen chairs and sighed loudly. "I didn't think my 'average' family could eat so much."

"You have to remember Greg."

"He does have an appetite, doesn't he. How much did he eat for breakfast? Was it four pieces of French toast or five?"

"I don't even want to think about it. It's bad enough to have to buy the size pot roast I did."

You mustn't forget, we'll be out of your house in a short time."

Sally stopped and looked around. The house was empty. It seemed to her that someone should be home. She took mental inventory: the kids were at the park, Donald was at work, and Roy was out running errands, but she had no idea where Greg was. He had no car; he hadn't mentioned going anywhere. Without saying anything to Heather, she went upstairs hoping to find him, maybe, taking a nap. Or maybe he went for a walk. Or maybe he went to the park with the kids. Yeah, that was it. He's fine.

Sally was about to turn around and go downstairs, but she passed her bedroom and there was a piece of paper and a small box on Roy's side of the bed. Cautiously, she approached the "gift" and found it was probably from Greg. But where was he? He was nowhere. But she wasn't going to panic. He actually belonged to Heather and Donald. She needed to know what was in the box. The neighbors are guests, she reasoned, but what if she just peeked. She couldn't help herself and decided to open the envelope. If she took it easy, she could re-seal the letter. The box wasn't sealed so no problem there.

Sally opened it by slitting the flap away from the rest of the envelope. She pulled the contents out and she settled down to read what was in it.

Dear Roy,

I believe the box holds our great grandfather's watch. Yes, I did say 'our' great-grandfather. Albert Carlson was his name, but I think you already know that. I'm sorry to say that I am very sneaky. I read through your notes on family, and it confirmed what I had, myself, learned. The watch I remember playing with as a child was not Alberts. That one was too precious to let anyone play with it. Great Grandma bought a cheap watch and let us have our fun with it, telling us all about Albert.

I was chosen as heir to the treasure, but, because of my health, I would make a poor safe house for it. The doctors have told me that I have cancer of the blood and will not live more than a few more months. That's why I'm giving this watch to you. I never married, I have no heir, whereas you

159

have a son and a daughter and Donald does not seem to be interested.

By the time you read this, I shall be far, far away and you have custody of the family treasure. Care for it well, tell your children about it.

Sincerely,

Greg

She mused the latest family history and was amazed. This means not only do we have a new cousin, but we have a new family next door that is related almost directly.

The latest addition to the treasures they had were odd: There was the watch, of course, but also a drawing done by Roy's great aunt Chloe when she was in kindergarten. There were tons of photos, a pair of ice skates that her cousin wore the time she tried out for the Olympics, and a box full of probably junk, such as a long-forgotten program when they went to the Ice Capades, oh, so many years ago.

Sally carefully folded the letter and slid it gingerly back into the aging envelope. Funny, she hadn't noticed the envelope's color and age before. Well, she must have been more interested in the contents instead of the medium. She put the letter and the box with the watch back as it was and left the room.

That night, after the kid's teeth-brushing, hair combing and lots of goodnight kisses, exhausted, Roy and Sally went to bed at the same time as their children. She had been waiting for him to open the envelope and the box, but he had just put them aside. Although disappointed, Sally reminded herself that there was a whole tomorrow waiting for her.

Chapter 16

It wasn't until mid-afternoon that Roy came into the living room holding the letter and box and practically shoved them into Sally's face.

"Look familiar?" he said.

Sally just looked at him but nodded.

"Do you know what's in it?"

Embarrassed, she nodded.

Roy withdrew the letter and box from Sally's face. She'd never seen anything like the expression he wore: a mix of curiosity, anger, and confusion. He tried to speak, but he just looked at her.

"What about the box and letter, Roy? My curiosity got the better of me and I read it, but I didn't look in the box. I think we have some talking to do."

He nodded and tried to clear his throat. Finally, he coughed and said a few words in "frog" voice.

"I can understand you now," she encouraged.

"I'm only thinking of you with this responsibility."

"Me?" she said with a voice half curiosity and half relief. "Me? He addressed it to you. Why do you think immediately of responsibility and not the honor of inheritance?"

"We must keep this thing safe. It's gotta be worth a lot."

"I only see it as a precious remembrance," Sally sighed.

"I think it's important to take this to someone who would appraise it. And I think it's worth quite a bit. We can put it in the safe, but it wouldn't be seen there, and it's a beautiful piece." Roy now had a look on his face of "Please don't say no."

Sally smiled. "I have a perfect place for it. I think I know a framer who can make up a respectful frame, and we can hang it above the fireplace in the kitchen."

Roy smiled. "Of course! We can hide it in plain sight! I'm betting that it won't be all that valuable."

"I bet it will, so it will be in a place where I seem to end up spending so much of my time. I can keep an eye on it.

Roy relaxed and smiled broadly.

* * * * *

It took a lot of mental headshaking, but Roy was finally able to get those scenes of the Chicago Fire out of his mind. He had picked up several books on the Eastland, which was strictly a Great Lakes vessel, and toyed with the pages of the first one, wondering why or how he should start. He had his characters in mind, the place where he would introduce them, and pretty much what they were going to say, but the whole thing seemed stilted and dry. He needed a bit of jazz to make it more interesting.

Just then, Sally ventured into his office, something she rarely did, but instead of wandering around a bit then coming up to his side offering her opinion, she flopped down on the couch and said nothing.

"Hi, Babe," he ventured. "Need something?"

She just quietly said, "No, thanks."

It looks like she needed a place to do some thinking, Roy thought. Looks as if she wants to be here and it is unlikely that she'll move. Best to get back to my intensions for the day before I run out of them.

Roy went back to work. The second line of the chapter needed something!

"Your script needs a bit of tuning, Roy."

Roy nearly jumped off the chair when Sally first spoke. He had not heard her get off the couch and stand in her comfortable position beside him.

The first sentence in his manuscript was dropped, and then he sat, chin in hand, wondering how to proceed.

"I just need this one sentence to make the introduction and I'll be able to proceed," he murmured to Sally.

"Then get to it, mister. I have a house to clean and a few smaller meals to fix. I can't stand here all day and tell you how to write your book."

That sounded more like Sally.

*　*　*　*　*

Joseph Erickson wanted certain things for his life, and in 1903, when the Eastland was...

*　*　*　*　*

"Oh, Roy, that is a horrible start. And you really want to have something in the book that even most Chicagoans don't remember?" Sally stared at him, and he returned the stare stubbornly.

"If the people of Chicago can't remember, this could be a great reminder," Roy finally answered. "Probably a better story than the, say, Iroquois Theater fire that happened around the same time. Besides, I already have two other

163

fires in this book." Roy got into his "writing position" and began pounding keys.

* * * * *

Joseph Erickson came to the United States for a better way of life as he saw it. For instance, in Sweden, low-ranking sailors would earn $3.00 per week, while in the US it was $1.75 per day. He knew he had to climb the ladder to become more, such as a captain, and recently it was declared that he had to be an American citizen as well.

Erickson wasn't justone of a few Scandinavians who left Norway or Sweden in favor of the new land. As it turned out, whole families emigrated as well as bachelors who were looking for opportunities and women to marry. By 1890, there were 2,200 Norwegians in Chicago alone.

But Joseph didn't come to the United States to marry. He came to become a "someone" in the shipping business. But in 1905 all he was qualified to do was to be an oiler, which he accepted. He was going to be the best oiler in the Michigan Steamship line.

* * * * *

"Roy, that is a clumsy way to open even just a paragraph," Sally almost whined.

Roy wished she would get out of his room when he had so much information to work with. Her interruptions were getting him nowhere."

"Can't you jazz it up a bit?"

Strange thing that he had thought that very word, and she had said it.

164

"I'll give it a go, Sweetheart. But I have been trying all afternoon to be jazzy. And this is where it's gotten me. Between the historical research and brief biographies of the people who really lived it, I can see where things must have shrunken to positive dullness."

"There's no alternative. Come on, Roy-boy, work on it, make it your own!" Sally cheered.

With Sally looking over his shoulder, he had no choice but to "jazz" things up a bit, so he did everything except pick up his trumpet and play a few bars.

He waited for her appraisal, but there was no response. Sally had gone, and he was free for now. Roy loved her dearly, but telling him how to write was a no-no. So, sans Sally, he took out portions of things he had written under her "tutelage." He kept the parts that made the story move, but strangely enough, when all those odd parts patched together, it actually sounded "jazzy." What a bonus!

* * * * *

By 1909, Joseph was known as "the high oiler," which meant he was ready to move up in the running of his current ship, the General Gillespie. He was on his way to becoming a nautical officer between his studies of engineering, and his intimate knowledge of every bolt and cranny on the Gillespie. He had what he needed: nautical knowledge and a recommendation letter from his captain who wrote:

This is to certify that the bearer, Joseph Mallings Erickson, has been employed on the US Dredge "General Gillespie" for four years, and I take great pleasure in recommending him to you as a sober, honest, industrious young man, and I consider him a very desirable citizen of the United States.

Very Respectfully

D.A. McDonald

Master, US Dredge, General Gillespie

It was a dangerous time to be on a steamboat. Too many boilers meant possible overheating explosions sending decks and passengers skyward. Another kind of almost disaster hit the Eastland when, in July of 1907, the ship began to tip one way, scaring the passengers so that they ran to the other side and had the same thing happen on the opposite side. Joseph Erickson herded a group of sailors to the main deck, who helped him to calm down the passengers and evened out the sides, so the ship steadied. Between 1825 and 1848, more than a thousand people were injured or killed by boiler failures. Mark Twain's brother, Henry Clemens, was killed on the Pennsylvania. It haunted the author the rest of his life.

With all the fatalities, the public seemed to forgive the Eastland started booking large groups of celebrants such as Western Electric's 2,500 bookings to cross Lake Michigan to South Haven for a huge picnic and games for all their employees. That was the mistake.

"What a morning this is!" Jennie Cech half spoke, half celebrated as she sat up in her bed and marveled at the azure sky. Thankful the clouds that threatened yesterday had gone, she just wanted that reassuring calmness and place to enjoy it. South Haven sounded like just the place. No congestion, no noises, no bad smells, and most of all, no Chicago River full of every kind of disgusting blob or swirl she could think of. It was too bad she had to board the Eastland there.

"Well," she thought, "I don't plan to go swimming in it. I am going to wait until we reach South Haven for that pleasure."

Jennie was quick with her lightly accented speech, enjoyed watching the boys gaze at her with their soft, dark eyes, and how they would quickly neaten their hair when she came

166

around. She wasn't terribly pretty, but as her father told her, she was "cute." She hated being "cute," so she dressed accordingly – as far away from cute as she could get. She looked older, but, no matter what, she was still her father's description.

Breakfast was waiting for her when she came downstairs, and she looked at the oatmeal with disgust. That was good enough for others who had also come from Sweden, but she was fully employed and brought her paycheck dutifully every week and gave it to her father. Therefore, she figured she should be given something else other than that gluey, hot cereal. Her mother agreed with Jennie, but it was Papa who ruled, especially when it came to money. He was determined to never let her roots be forgotten, and cereal was part of those roots.

She ate her oatmeal dutifully.

Jennie was looking forward to the steamship trip to South Bend and a party full of the kind of food that the people from Sweden had never heard of much less tasted. She had even been asked by her director to help her countrymen to identify what was in the pots and dishes on the buffet table as they passed down the line. Jennie hoped she herself could figure out what food was in what dish.

The trip to South Bend was on a steamship called the Eastland, and Jennie had dressed in something that she concluded was "nautical" and somewhat "jaunty." Many of the planned games after a huge banquet of all-you-can-eat lunches were partner games. She had decided that she would play games with as many different male partners as she could. Later, when the evening started showing its shadows, she would dance with as many different partners as she had at the games. Jennie wondered how many of those partners would remember her on Monday morning.

167

"Jennie!" her mother said with a bit of alarm, it's time to go! You don't want to miss the boat, do you?"

"It didn't take Jennie long to grab her bag, containing her swimming clothes, and the package of food she and her mother had made as her lunch contribution.

It wasn't far to the docks, but it also wasn't the friendliest way to go. The closer she got to the docks; the more rough-and-tumble were the surroundings. Knowing this, her father walked the ten blocks to the waterfront with her.

"Papa, look! There's my ship, the Eastland!

"Yes, daughter, I can see. Such a beauty! So tall! How in the world are you going to get to the top so you can be on deck?'

"There is a new invention on the ship. It's amazing. It's called 'stairs.'"

Jennie looked at her father as his face turned from "I'm concerned" to "I've been had." Both laughed raucously.

"I best be getting on my way. The ship will be putting out in about twenty minutes, and I need time to see everything from as high as I can." She quickly kissed her father, turned, and ran toward the ship. That was the last time he ever saw her.

Jennie checked in at the gate and received her room assignment. She would be sharing her cabin with two other women that she didn't know very well, Ellie Carlson and Oma Dorph. They weren't expected to stay on the ship until the next day, but the three-hour trip back to Chicago usually found people napping anywhere they could find comfortable. Pickpockets somehow always managed to get in, and they were just waiting for the time when even their hands couldn't rouse passengers. Therefore, allowing people to lock their cabins prevented all that.

Jennie excitedly dropped off her bag in her cabin, and then she added her food to the mile-long table that was set up for lunch. Dinner was a sit-down affair served by the ship's staff. She quickly walked to the stairs and began to climb. It was a chore. And the closer she got to the top deck, the more sway the ship had.

As soon as she was at the top, she almost ran to the railing, but she put on the brakes as soon as she got close enough to the rail. It was the highest Jennie had ever been. Taking steps slowly and lightly, she approached the edge as if it were a sleeping tiger.

Almost at the railing, she heard a shout. Jennie turned and looked and could easily see it was no passenger, but rather, a man in uniform who shouted again, "More people on the port side needed."

She could see the confused looks on the people who had no idea what a "port" side meant but rather followed the crowds. Jennie was one who didn't know the term for the left side of the ship but followed the others. That's when she realized how much the Eastland had dipped toward the other ship tied up on the right side of the Eastland.

The ship again leaned, but this time on the right, toward the pier. And shouts raised the orders to go to the port side. This time Jennie was shouted at to go to the starboard. She still didn't know what "starboard" or "port" meant, so she just followed the crowd.

It was too much.

Jennie felt like she was floating on air as the Eastland twisted slightly and dipped farther and farther into the disgusting water of the Chicago River. Jennie's reality came back to her the instant the ship hit the water which she hit full in the face so hard it took her breath from her. She tried to get a gulp of air, but instead she ingested a gulp of the river and quickly threw up. The more she tried to clear her lungs, the more she swallowed followed by more vomiting.

* * * * * *

"Roy! Don't write that! I like Jennie, and you are going to kill her off, aren't you?"

"Hush, Sally. I'm on a roll. Don't take me away from the scene!"

Sally huffed and stomped out of Roy's' office. Roy didn't change his mind.

* * * * * *

Finally, Jennie got her stomach to settle a bit, but now, how was she supposed to get out of the water. Even though she could swim, she had never tried to swim in a garbage dump like the Chicago River until now. With oil from the ship, she found swimming was nearly impossible. The water again covered her face as she went down face up. Jennie tried to call for help, but her throat was too slick with oil, and rinsing would have caused her to get rid of more river garbage, so she decided that she would just let whatever God had in mind for her to happen. The only thing she could do was to float, face down in the muck. It became more and more difficult to get her head out of the water to get a good long gasp of air. She was floating deeper and deeper into the river, and, somehow, she didn't care anymore. She was ready to sleep.

Jennie felt an annoying tug on her left arm and tried to let the tugger know she just wanted to be left alone. But it didn't stop. Someone wanted her to come out of the water and through the floating mass of garbage, but, because of the oil, he had a hard time hanging onto her slickery arm.

Finally, he got her out of the water and another man joined him to carry her onto the grass where the doctors and nurses were waiting for her. Jennie took a good lungful of air and was surprised that it was clean, and she didn't feel like coughing

Suddenly, Jennie was alone. She didn't want to be alone. She had her full faculties now, where was that darling man that had saved her from drowning? She had to see him just once more to thank him, but he was gone. She tried to sit up but found her legs were too weary, so she calmed down.

"We mustn't move around so much, dear. Your body took a lot of punishment this morning."

Jennie looked up to see a woman about her mother's age wearing a nurse's cap. She tried to tuck Jennie into the makeshift bed, but Jennie was having none of it.

"I've got to get up and find the man who pulled me out of the water. Do you know who it was?"

"No, dear, I saw no one with you. It was just you struggling to sit up. I'm from the hospital across the city. A lot of us got called out when the ship turned over."

"It turned over? Is that why I ended up in the water? I imagine I wasn't the only one who got wet. Are there any others like me?"

"Many. And my name is Nora. When I got here, I was told I was to be a 'mama' to all the women who were fortunate to survive the Chicago River."

"I guess I didn't do very well in that department. I remember throwing up a lot."

"That's where you saved yourself. If it hadn't been for the garbage that made you sick, you would be dead by now."

"Nora, do you mean people actually died for swallowing that junk?"

Nora nodded. "Your body was smart enough to know to purge itself. And you were smart enough to let it."

"I'd like to talk about the man who pulled me out. All I can remember is that..."

"He probably looked like just about any young man who volunteered to help. And there were dozens of them. My advice is to let go of him and concentrate on something like your job.

Jennie nodded, and Nora headed off to find her something to make her vomit some more so that the last little bit wouldn't poison her. But Jennie got a look at his face. It was a quick look, but enough to be able to affirm him among a dozen young men.

She was feeling much better. The vomiting had stopped, and all she wanted to do was to get a bath and then some sleep. She could walk home.

Nora appeared again, but this time she agreed that this was a good time for Jennie to go home. One less patient wouldn't do herself any harm.

But out of the big nowhere, on the way home, there was her savior, the man who pulled her out. His clothing was torn and full of oil, and he was looking just as she was sure she was. He was blonde, though hard to see blonde when covered with oil, he had clear blue eyes and a small mouth and was wearing what used to be an officer's coat.

About to go over and tap him on the shoulder, Jennie was interrupted by her mother. "Mama!" What are you doing here? Where's Papa?"

"I told him I would go and find you."

"Mama, you look funny. You're so pale. What's wrong?"

"We heard about the Eastland, and he was about to go look for you, but he sat down in the rocking chair and said he didn't feel well."

Jennie turned as white as her mother.

"He had a heart attack. Jennie, I'm afraid he's gone."

About two moments later, Jennie and her mother turned and made a beeline for the house.

*   *   *   *   *   *

Roy stopped and stared at the page.

"Well, come on, Roy," Sally said making Roy practically jump out of his seat.

After a second of gathering his cool, he told her she surprised him. "I had no clue you were anywhere near me. And reading my material over my shoulder when the ink wasn't even dry is dirty pool."

"I just wanted to know what's happening with Jennie and Joseph."

He looked at her straight in the eye and said, "Give me about ten minutes and I can tell you."

"Are you going to have the two meet?"

"Hah! Wouldn't you like to know!"

"Yes, I would."

"What exactly do you want to know?"

"Do they ever meet? Does she go back to work at Western Electric? What could have happened to Jennie and her mother? What was the end story on the Eastland? Did Joseph get another ship? Where did the..."

"Enough! There's enough information needed to write another book. I can't use all of that. I will let a few things slip, but I want to leave facts hanging so enough readers' curiosity will spur them to the library to quench their need for an ending. It will keep people remembering my book. Since both characters were real, there would be plenty of info on Joseph, but I'm afraid Jennie did get the short end of the stick. She was one of many anonymous passengers who were pulled to safety. But I have a splendid idea: why don't you go away, and I'll tie up some of those ends for you."

Sally caught the gleam in his eye and feigned innocent agreement.

"Oh, yes sir!" she wailed in a southern accent. "I must not take any more of your valuable time. Your book is far more important than I am."

Once she was gone, Roy had a bunch of research to do. He didn't want to write all that much more, but he had to have his facts straight. One piece of information that he was sure Sally wouldn't like at all, but it had to be told. Other than taking no liberties with the story of the Eastland, and the four hundred and eighty-eight souls it took, the only fantasy he perpetrated was the one about Jennie and Joseph. Each one was true to history with one little exception: Jennie was pulled to safety by a young man, yes, but it wasn't Joseph. Joseph was down below hoping to keep his own life intact when someone pulled him out. He had almost died. He never would have had the wherewithal to pull Jennie out of the river's muck.

So, he wrote.

It seemed that the City of Chicago and anyone who had anything to do with the Eastland was investigated, Joseph

Erickson included. Joseph was called to be a witness, but way before he was put under oath, he knew that if he was convicted of even a minor role, he would never be hired to work on a ship again. The rest of Joseph's story he left at that turning point to allow his readers to research it or just leave it where it was.

Jennie Cech deemed it much too disgusting to mourn her father while she was still covered in the residue of the river. As soon as she got home, she swept through the living room with only a glance at her father, stretched out on the couch with his arms crossed over his chest. Once her bathing was completed, she put on fresh-smelling clothes, and even a smidge of cologne to get the memory of the scent of the day. Now she could properly mourn. Since the funeral was to be held in the home as was the custom of the day, Jennie had much to do, and she had to take care of Mama, too.

After being told that her job was still hers, Jennie had to think about it first. She finally concluded that, other than booking the trip on the wrong ship, the company was not to blame as to what happened. She returned to her job.

She worked at Western Electric for a few more years, but she had met, as she put it, the perfect man. It was a good alliance, and they stayed together for almost fifty years. Yes, occasionally, she did think of that man that pulled her out of the river, the one with bright eyes, the strong arm, and the satisfied smile. But that was only occasionally. One morning on her way to the library where she worked now that her three children had grown up, she was thinking about something else when she smacked into the open door of an automobile. A man got out of the car and asked her if she was all right. She said she was so clumsy and please forgive her.

When she looked into his eyes, she knew him. It was 1915 all over again, and there was Joseph. He tipped his hat again, apologized then sped off in his car. Jennie shook her head. It could not have been Joseph.

"Or could it?" Roy said with a sly smile on his face.

Chapter 17

It wasn't until almost 10:00 AM the following morning that Roy wobbled into the kitchen muttering, "Where the hell is the coffee?" Sally was glad that he had gotten so much sleep that she didn't mind the epithet. When he had gotten all his notes together and started to compile the book, it usually meant he had slept many extra hours. But in this case, Sally didn't think so. At least not every day for weeks. But he did anyway.

The books and articles he had read were coming together, according to Roy, and they continued to fascinate him. Once he had his coffee, he turned into the writing machine that Sally hated. It was nothing but mishmash at that stage of the game, but she knew it would be just fine eventually. She loved to read what he had written that day so they could discuss it over dinner. But even Roy realized at this date it was too loose to have anything to say. He struggled to get even one chapter into a readable state, so they had something to talk about.

This time the book was about the dying Irish because the failure of the potato crop. There were several main characters, depending on what phase of the voyage was being discussed, lack of harvest, help from other countries, or the voyage itself.

Despite his notes, his thinking on what he had so far was quite good, and Sally allowed Roy all the explanations he needed to clarify all the situations the participants found themselves wrapped in. It caused not only the hunger and disease that was so widely known, but it caused hopelessness, families being torn apart as some went to the United States, and the participants that stayed in Ireland because of the disease. The deaths were too terrible and communicable to take on ships. When the potato crop failed it not only spawned a disease, but the Irish found themselves without out the nutritious source they had come to rely on and a revenue source that they found to be irreplaceable. A failure of the potato crop was something that they knew might happen, which it did many times in the nineteenth century, with not the lesser failure of 1846-7.

In the 1840's, the potato's nutritional value was known to be higher than that of corn or grains. It included a healthy number of calories plus vitamins, especially vitamin C, protein, potassium, magnesium, calcium, and iron. Potatoes were very digestible and proved it by the rare showing of gastrointestinal problems associated with the Irish peasantry.

The ease of cooking was also a plus. They could be steamed, boiled or even roasted over an open flame. Lately, however, a new way of preparing potatoes was becoming more popular. The boiled potatoes were mixed with butter and milk then crushed. From there the preparer would stir the mixture until the it was a lumpless mass, and in the end, the mass was served as something called "mashed potatoes."

"So, you can see how important potatoes are to the Irish. Take them away, and they have nothing to eat that can replace it." Roy sat back in his chair, burped quietly and smiled generously.

"But that was back in the 1840's. Has there been another between then and now?" Sally asked.

"Not really. At least I don't think so. This one was big enough to do it for Ireland."

"What about all the other countries that got their goods from Ireland?"

"They figured it out – and don't ask me how! -- that the importing the potato from Ireland was the culprit. No more imports showed no more plague."

Sally had a confused look on her face.

"What?" Roy said with a touch of annoyance.

You see, um, well, there seems to be a lot of missing parts to your story. And your explanation seems a bit, uh, wanting."

"Wanting?! Missing parts?! Well, I can see your mind is closed. I have a ton of 'missing parts' that you should know about before you made such a judgement."

Roy's anger scared Sally and she withdrew by picking up the morning paper and turning her back on him.

Actually, he was not mad at all. It appeared that he just wanted to get a little movement and spark in the morning. When she turned back to see if he was still there, she caught the sneaky smile and devil in his expression.

"Oh, you!" she replied and threw a pen at him.

"So sorry, Gal Pal Sal," a name he used when he was overly sorry, "but I just needed to get a rise out of you. You look like you need one."

"I do?"

"Yeah. I gave you a good opening for a comeback, but you ignored it. I guess I just needed to know if you were okay."

She picked up another pen and this time aimed and whipped it at him. It hit him in the neck.

"Ow! Sal don't do that anymore! I don't know how I'm going to explain that mark to others."

"Oh, come on! That pen couldn't weigh more than two ounces." She reached out and touched the spot where the

179

pen had hit. "There isn't even a bit of red there. "The only explanation I need to give anyone is, 'It's none of your business'. And speaking of 'business,' I'd still like to know about the frequency of the potato famines.

"Okay, back to business. But I don't know why you want to know these things. They're just numbers," Roy reminded her.

"Ah, yes," Sally reminded him right back. "Put together with words and they can make a mighty statement."

"All right! You want words? I'll give you plenty of words along with the numbers."

"Great! This makes me feel like a sleuth. Maybe we can solve this mess before the author does."

"Sal, I've written a ton of mysteries, and you have shown no interest in them or the outcome. Why now?"

"Because this is real. It happened and it happened to our family." She sat down on the couch in his office, the one he napped on frequently.

"Okay, Sherlock. You asked for it!"

For the next hour, Roy gave her the synopsized version of all he had picked up during his months on the project. Sally scribbled all she could on a legal pad and somehow managed to keep up with him.

"Now comes the part you asked for. You ready?"

Sally nodded and readied her pen.

He began with stats of a regular position and went into what would happen in a disaster situation.

"I'm sure you're aware that the potato cannot be canned, salted or cured, so the peasant farmer lives from crop to crop. Lucky for him, it coincided with the June, July and August meal crop, called 'the meal months' so they had something to eat. The crop was the only thing to eat, and it was bought from stores on blinding cost. If this was not in their budget, they lived in a state of hunger until their potato crop had been harvested. But worse, if their crop failed, they had nothing to eat. And if the crop was subpar for two years in a row, the only thing that they had that was sure was starvation. The crop of 1845 was partially blighted followed by 'An Gorta Mor'—the Great Hunger—when the crop of 1846 – 1847 was blighted. The nineteenth century gave the people who lived on the potato crop failure in 1800, 1818, 1821, 1830, 1833, 1835,1839, and 1842.

"In 1846, Sir Robert Peel imported Indian corn and other rough grains for the families for relief. After the potato, these rough foods, which took much grinding, were very difficult to adjust to.

"Father Mathew, the local priest who was very popular with the peasant class, was invited to give testimony at the House of Lords in 1847. His speech came down to one sentence: 'I do not think that the people of Ireland will ever again depend upon the potato crop',"

Sally sat, pen still poised, looking at Roy as if he were a statue.

Roy could see she had a multitude of questions, but she didn't say anything for a good long time. Finally, she seemed to snap back into reality.

"Why didn't you tell me this before?" Sally said with part pity in her voice and part accusation. What's going on with their potato crop this year? What can we do to help them?"

"Father Mathew and other volunteer workers strained to save the people of Cork with no government relief in sight. Operating a soup kitchen almost alone near his house, feeding between five and six thousand a day, Mathew paid half expenses from his meager savings and the rest from contributions. The soup kitchen closed, but the gifts of food didn't: food was distributed from his house at any hour. Fighting depression and exhaustion, Mathew gave out food no matter what the time of day or night.

"He also established a Catholic cemetery where Mathew presided over funerals. During March and April,1847, he buried what he estimated to be 36 souls per day. Between November 1846 and June, 1847, it was thought that 6,000 to 10,000 were buried. The rest of Ireland was no better off than Cork. It was evident that March of 1847 was the worst of all so far. Limerick reported that starving people were tearing at the barks of trees off and eating it raw. Then there were those poor souls who were almost mad with hunger that collected raw seaweed and ate it that way.

"It wasn't long before more than 5,000 ships loaded with passengers that were anxious to leave the utter destruction of their home country were aboard. The Jamestown was the first to travel with it food and supplies bound for Ireland. It didn't seem to matter where the barrels came from, tiny frontier towns or great cities. They all donated what they could."

Roy stopped for a minute to catch his own breath when he saw Sally was having trouble breathing combined with weeping. He left his desk, cradled her heaving torso, and tried to sooth her. It worked, and the erratic breathing calmed, and the tears started to dry.

"Why didn't you tell me it was so horrid?" she said as she looked up at him with her eyes starting to glaze over again.

"I thought you understood it was ghastly," Roy said softly. "If it made you this upset, I think I got my message across."

Sally sniffled back a tear and snuggled into his arms.

"By the way," Roy was about to ask. It made her happy to hear him talk in his everyday voice. He looked deeply into her eyes, kissed her and asked,

"What's for dinner?"

* * * * *

Dinner was a quick thing that night. Not for lack of food, but for lack of time. Sally was so delighted to have Roy back after having immersed himself in facts and other minutia for so long, she was going to take himself any way he wanted. She told herself she should be used to it by now, but somehow the comeback was still a thrill.

"You presented so many possibilities for being the lost relative in the Boston story," Sally pointed out, "that this time I have to ask who was your relative?"

Roy looked down at his spoon, picked it up, and shined it with his napkin. Sally had to know, but suddenly she was sorry she did. He seemed almost hurt.

"It's hard to explain. It's one of those relational situations that gets awfully twisted," his downcast face suddenly made a cheerier comeback, and he began to explain. "I didn't even use his name this time because he was a victim of the flood."

"Oh, I'm so sorry. If you'd rather not talk about it, I can understand..."

"No, no," he said with a wry smile. "It's not that, it's just that most people don't believe me. His name was Tim Stoddard, and he was sort of my cousin. In a time when people still left unwanted children on someone's doorstep, Tim was one of them. My great Aunt Flora and Uncle James adopted him. He was my dad's buddy. I never got to meet him as he almost died in the 1919 Molasses Flood. He was, as Great Aunt

183

Flora called him, he was 'damaged goods.' He was never the same after the flood, which is understandable, and he died of his injuries in about 1932."

"Did anyone ever figure out who his real parents were?"

"No, Sal, in those days, a child on a doorstep meant God was asking for your help, and in some places it was mandatory. And yet, in other places, raising a foundling was a shame. Go figure.

"Have you got any pictures?"

"Yeah," Roy said with a huge sigh. In that box on the bottom shelf by the fireplace. I don't have all that many pictures, maybe three or four."

Dinner was forgotten and Sally went right to the pictures. "Oh, look at this one, Roy, he's playing 'Cowboy'. All he needed was a horse."

"He had a horse," Roy said, sitting down in front of the fireplace." My uncle and aunt had a ranch, and he was taught the right way to ride. Too bad he was injured. He couldn't ride after that. Even after his injury, my dad loved to be around him. He learned Tim's way of 'hand talking' as he called it."

"Look at this picture, Roy! The way he scrunched up his face he looked just like my sister Annie."

"Sally, are you saying that you think Tim could be your uncle?"

She just looked at him and wagged her head vigorously.

"Well, we can dream, can't we?" Roy philosophized.

Chapter 18

It was 12:41 PM on January 15,1919, when Antonio crouched behind the massive molasses tank, so he had a good view of Antonio's sister, Lucita, as she was being scolded by two adults. The children had all been told to collect wood from around the tank and bring it to school. Two railroad workers wagged their fingers at Lucita and soon began to shout at her to get out of there. Antonio came out of hiding. Everything happened fast.

Something rose up from behind Lucita, and the railroad men stopped yelling at her and just watched what was happening, their mouths agape. The terror on the men's faces caused Antonio to turn around. He saw a shadow falling over Lucita.

*   *   *   *   *

Peter backed up his team to the Bay State Railroad shed and presented the clerk with a bill of lading. He had just picked up fifteen hogs and was now delivering them. The two men took some time out of their schedules to talk, and that's when Peter felt it: a shake of the ground followed by a roar. He was convinced it was a Commercial Street elevated train that had jumped the tracks and tumbled to the street below. A second later, he wished it was what happened.

*   *   *   *   *

George Scott, who was a U.S. Navy gunner's mate, stood on the Bessie J.'s deck, and chatted with two other sailors about their work that they said they had completed that morning. They had been stripping small boats of their ordnance and armaments. Since the Great Conflict was over, wartime identification was no longer needed.

They decided to take a break for lunch when George Scott heard a rumble and began shouting at the top of his lungs.

* * * * *

Benjamin, 20, was a freight clerk for the Boston & Maine Railroad company. As he walked by the Number Three freight shed on the Commercial Street wharf, he could make out Liam, a deaf-mute laborer who worked for the railroad. He was stacking crates, preparing them for shipment. Benjamin didn't envy him, unable to hear or make a single sound. Oh, he was a hard worker but could never join in the fun and gossip with the others on the docks. And that was Walter's favorite part of work.

Benjamin paused at the doorway. Liam looked up. It was that second when Benjamin heard a rumbling, like a passing train over Commercial Street except much, much louder.

It was then that something happened that Walter would never forget. Liam pointed a finger in Walter's direction, but beyond that. And the one who never made a sound let go with a screech so loud it seemed to cleave through Benjamin's soul.

With unbelievable strength, the molasses burst from its tank prison. Each direction shot pieces of the tank as if out of a cannon. Fastening bolts became bullets that sped through the air in every point of the compass.

Horses died by the dozen, and humans suffered the same fate. To free those who were trapped, police and firemen worked until they gave out. Sailors off the Nantucket and the Bessie J shored up the work of the first responders, but many couldn't be saved, including Antonio's sister Lucita. The question quickly rose: what was beyond repair, and how many people had been saved and how many were not. Elevator train passenger Martin Soffer whose train was just coming into the wreckage area when he pulled the emergency cord about three train cars ahead of the debris when a molasses wave hit the tracks. Had Martin waited a moment more to pull the cord, it was likely the whole train would have plunged off the tracks. As if it weren't enough, Martin climbed back on the tracks and went as far as he could to warn a train coming from the north that the track was down.

Chapter 19

"There were many stories of heroism, neglect, deaths and saves that day," Roy concluded, "but I don't think I can remember half of them. At least not without some of the records I did find. I've often wondered if it had been a hurricane and the ocean sent in waves, trains came tumbling off the tracks, and took buildings with it, would there be more about the disaster?"

"Just the concept of the thing is horrible, but somehow, I can't help but giggle." Sally insisted. "Maybe, if it had been cement raining down or something serious like that, but molasses? Come on, that must be worth at least a concealed snort or two."

"Don't forget that twenty-one people died."

"Was your relative on the obituary list?"

"If he was, then I wouldn't be here."

"Oh, yeah. Well, which one was it? The guy who stopped the incoming train?"

"No one so glamorous, sorry. It was a young student who got stuck in a pool of molasses. Once the molasses began to harden, without help, he was there to stay."

"Well, obviously, he got help."

Roy laughed. "Yes, but that alone was a disaster."

"Now I have got to hear the end of this one. Come on, how did they get him out?" Sally demanded.

They found him in the wee hours of the next day up to his hips in stiff molasses. The only thing they could do other than chip him out was to spread boiling water around him.

They had been using hot water to keep town entrances open. So, they used it, probably burned him quite a bit, but it worked, sort of. His body was willing to get out of the mess, but not his clothes. You see, he was up to his waist in it."

"And?"

"Think about it a minute," Roy encouraged.

Sally began to giggle, then stopped herself.

"Yes," Roy agreed. "I can see how that would be funny. And sad."

"Well, now who is going to star in your next chapter?"

"Are you kidding? I'm done with this book. I don't know of any more that could belong to it."

"But you're skipping the whole twentieth century!" Sally said in disappointment.

Maybe my grandson can carry on. If you remember, I said I wanted to write about those events that most people have forgotten about or never heard of in the first place."

"What about the birth of Jesus?" Sally challenged. "Couldn't have been any event more famous."

"Don't challenge me or I'll delete the part I wrote about your great aunt."

"Aunt Maddie? There's nothing interesting about her!"

"How about her crocheting? All the messages she left for people in her work when she died."

"She just wanted people to remember her and to remind them what she tried to teach them," Sally said firmly.

"You're being very charitable. Don't you remember what she crocheted in your doily?'

"Of course I remember. She said 'Messy.' And she should. But I've cleaned up my act." Sally smiled behind her hand.

But no matter. I'm going to leave Aunt Maddie and the other doily-receivers alone. My grandson..."

"Or granddaughter." Sally gently reminded him.

"Of course. One of them will write all about things that have happened in the Twentieth Century that have the 'Canardly' seal of approval. Who knows where this could lead? One of our grandchildren could write about the twenty-first century, our great-great grandchild the twenty-second, and so on. Every hundred years they would have to expand the book."

"And I'll be waiting for my chance to steal this manuscript for a good read-through," Sally assured him.

They settled on the couch, each one with their magazine. Suddenly, Sally sat straight up and said, "Ohmygosh!" I forgot about dinner! It's still on the stove!"

"Messy," Roy said and wagged his head. "Very messy."

"It's not, and you know it," Sally countered. When she got to the kitchen, she was relieved when she saw it wasn't a total loss. It was one of Roy's favorites, an Italian-style casserole with rotini and cellentani in her home-made sauce with mini-meatballs.

"Maybe one of your Italian relatives ate something like this," Sally suggested as she set the table.

"My Italian ancestors had been long gone from Italy before pasta came along," Roy informed her proudly as he filled the water glasses. "You must read the book before you can really understand what I mean. I'll give you a copy after dinner."

"Good deal!"

Sally ate quickly and started clearing the table before Roy had finished. He grabbed his plate before she could get away with it.

"Hey, hey, hey! Wait a minute! I know you're anxious to get to the book, but not at the expense of my stomach."

"Well, can't you put a little spin on it?"

After the dishes were done, Sally sat in the living room anxiously waiting for Roy to come back with the copy. He was agonizingly slow. Finally, after a half an hour, he appeared with the manuscript.

"Now you know that I always depend on your opinion, so read it well so we can talk it over," he instructed shaking the papers in her face. She was just afraid of the whole thing coming apart as he shook it. It didn't happen.

Sally put out her hands and took the papers. "Now I'll be able to find out who Antonio, and Johnny, and Minnie were. This is going to be fun. Have you decided on a title yet?"

"I'm leading toward "The Canardly." What do you think?"

"Well," she said thoughtfully, "That's great for you and I who know the joke, but nobody else will."

"I wrote about the joke in the first chapter. And besides, if it's a puzzle to others, they might want to understand what the title means and buy it."

"Hmmm, could work. Well, you're the author. It's up to you."

"When you finish reading it, maybe you'll have another suggestion.

Sally brought her feet up on the sofa and sat on them: her favorite reading position. It was a little past midnight when she yawned her way to bed. Roy was already asleep.

Morning came and Roy had been up by five. He had made coffee and was on his third cup when Sally surprised him by getting up at six. Roy speculated that she was anxious to talk about the book. She wasn't. In fact, she ignored him altogether. He took this as a sign that the book was subpar.

"Sal Pal, are you in there?" he asked her softly.

"Where's the coffee?"

"I made some earlier. The pot is still hot."

She wandered over to the counter, opened the cabinet to find her cup, banged it down, yawned, poured a cup and sipped it.

"You make lousy coffee," she told him. Suddenly she perked up, smiled, raised her cup and said, "But you write fabulous books!"

After that they talked all morning. Oh, Sally had suggestions, and Roy agreed with some of them. But best of all, she knew who all those characters were she had heard about for months.

* * * * *

Two weeks after "The Canardly" hit the shelves, the news was astoundingly good, and the book was off to an auspicious start.

Roy had finished talking to his agent about further publicity and was bubbling over with news. "Aaron just told me that they want to send me to England to participate in the London Book Fair! It's one of the most prestigious in the world, and I'm going to be a part of it! Isn't that fabulous?"

She didn't look happy.

"And you're going too!"

"You remembered!

"Yup! So, you can cross off London on your bucket list.

"You're going to have to translate the meaning of the title a lot."

Roy shook his head. "No, I've decided to let their curiosity sell the books. I'm going to tell them that discovering what the title means is part of the fun."

"What would I do without you?! With all the nationalities that make you, I have my very own canardly. But which one do I love the best? I canardly tell.